OCEAN CITY MIDNIGHTS

CLAUDIA VANCE

CHAPTER ONE

Matt and Lauren exchanged glances as they climbed the steps of Starfish Cove Inn, both absorbing the reality that this off-season job would be unlike anything either had experienced before.

"Are we really cut out for this?" Lauren asked as Matt paused before opening the front door.

Matt shrugged. "I guess we'll find out soon enough."

Inside, Travis and Kelly greeted them, their faces bright with relief.

"You two are lifesavers," Kelly said. "The kids' schedules are getting more hectic by the day, and we've been desperate for reliable help."

Travis nodded. "Seriously, thank you both for agreeing to this. Having you here until March means we can actually have some family time this fall and winter."

The inn looked different today. Boxes of fall decorations sat open in the lobby, and the smell of cinnamon and cloves wafted through the air. The historic charm of the place was undeniable, from the original hardwood floors to the antique furniture that made visitors feel like they'd stepped back in time.

"We should probably start with the complete tour," Kelly said. "I know you've both been here before, but running the place is a different story."

Just then, a sleek black cat jumped onto the reception desk, her tail swishing back and forth as she surveyed the newcomers.

"And this," Travis said, reaching out to scratch behind the cat's ears, "is our newest staff member. Meet Binx."

"She showed up on our doorstep about a month ago," Kelly explained. "The guests adore her."

Matt stepped forward, extending his hand toward Binx. The cat immediately perked up, leapt gracefully onto Matt's shoulder, and settled around his neck like a furry scarf.

"Well, that's unusual," Travis said with a laugh. "Binx typically takes her time warming up to new people."

"Do you worry about guests with allergies?" Lauren asked as she watched Matt continue to pet the contented cat.

Travis shook his head. "We mention her presence on the booking site, and we keep her out of two of the rooms, which are specifically set aside for guests with allergies. So far, it's worked out perfectly."

"She seems to know exactly which guests to approach and which to avoid," Kelly added. "It's like she can sense who has allergies."

"Smart cat," Travis said with a nod. "Now, let's get started with the tour. We've got a lot to cover."

They began in the lobby, where Travis showed them the ancient computer system they used for the bookings. The main reception area featured a grand oak desk with intricate carvings along its edges, worn smooth by decades of guests checking in and out. Above the reception desk hung a large preserved starfish in an ornate shadow box frame. "That's our namesake," Travis explained, noticing Lauren's gaze. "Edward Matthews, who built this place in 1912, found it on the beach. It's been watching over guests ever since."

Running his hand along the polished surface of the desk, Travis continued, "This desk has been here since the inn opened. It's seen more history than all of us combined."

The lobby walls featured framed black-and-white photographs showing Ocean City in the early 1900s—pictures of the boardwalk with women in long dresses and men in formal suits, the beach dotted with old-fashioned umbrellas and bathing costumes.

In the corner stood a magnificent grandfather clock, its pendulum swinging with a hypnotic rhythm. The steady *tick-tock* created a soothing background soundtrack to the space.

Kelly pulled out a leather-bound ledger from a drawer in the reception desk. "And this is our backup for bookings. The computer system crashes more often than we'd like to admit. The ledger has saved us more than once. We're finally getting an upgrade in the spring, but I still recommend keeping this handy."

Travis motioned for them to follow him through a set of double doors with etched glass panels. "Let's head to the front porch first, then we'll work our way around."

The wraparound porch was one of the inn's most distinctive features. It extended along the entire front and both sides of the building, offering different perspectives of Ocean City. The white-painted wooden railings contrasted beautifully with the sage-green exterior of the inn. Comfortable rocking chairs and wicker seating arrangements were positioned strategically to take advantage of the views.

"This is where guests spend most of their time in good weather," Travis said as they walked along the porch's wooden planks, which creaked pleasantly underfoot. "We serve coffee and tea out here in the mornings. The sunrise view from the east side is spectacular."

The porch ceiling was painted a soft pale blue, with hanging ferns and potted mums in fall colors adding touches of natural beauty to the space.

"We're planning to add more heaters so guests can enjoy the porch even in cooler weather," Kelly explained, pointing to the existing propane heaters positioned between seating areas.

They continued their tour, moving next through the dining room, where breakfast would be served each morning. The room featured several mismatched antique tables and chairs along with one long farmhouse table that anchored the center of the space, somehow creating a cohesive, charming atmosphere. Wrought iron pendant lights hung from the high ceiling, casting a warm glow over the room, and built-in china cabinets displayed vintage teacups and serving pieces.

"We keep it simple but quality," Travis explained. "Fresh baked goods, fruit, eggs, and coffee. The recipes are all here." He handed Lauren a worn binder. "My grandmother's secret recipes. Don't lose this, or she'll haunt us all."

Lauren flipped through the pages, noting the handwritten notes in the margins. "These look delicious." She passed the binder to Matt, who studied a few pages with interest.

"I've always wanted to do a little more baking," Matt said, reading a recipe for blueberry scones.

Kelly smiled. "Perfect! We were hoping you both would handle the cooking. Most guests rave about our breakfasts. It's what keeps them coming back."

"We can definitely manage this together," Lauren said, looking at Matt with newfound excitement.

"And in the afternoon, we put out cheese and fruit platters, fresh cookies, and hot drinks," Travis added. "It's the little touches that make people feel at home."

Next, they explored the inn's library, a cozy room with floor-to-ceiling bookshelves and a fireplace flanked by worn leather armchairs. The shelves were packed with everything from beach reads to historical fiction and local-interest books.

"This is where guests tend to gather on rainy days or in the evenings," Kelly said, adjusting a stack of board games on a small table in the corner. "We keep the fire going from October through March."

The library had a distinctly masculine feel with its deep-green walls, mahogany woodwork, and brass reading lamps. A painting of a rough-looking fisherman hung above the fireplace, while an old scientific chart showing different mollusks completed the nautical theme.

"Most of these books have been donated by guests over the years," Travis mentioned. "Some people leave behind what they've finished reading, and others bring books specifically for our collection. We've got quite a library of signed first editions now."

A hidden door in the library's paneling led to a small study. "This used to be the original owner's private office," Kelly explained as they entered the intimate space. "Now it's a quiet workspace for guests who need to check in with the office while they're staying with us."

The study featured a compact writing desk, a comfortable office chair, and a small love seat under the window. In the corner, a tripod held an antique telescope pointed toward the ocean.

After exploring the main floor, they headed toward the rear of the inn, where French doors opened onto the garden. The backyard was a hidden oasis, surrounded by a white picket fence draped with climbing roses, now mostly dormant for the season. Stone pathways wound through garden beds filled with native perennials and ornamental grasses swaying in the autumn breeze.

"I can tell this is magical in the summer," Lauren said, taking in the serene space.

"It's beautiful year-round," Kelly replied. "The garden has something to offer in every season." She pointed to several seating areas nestled throughout the space—a wrought iron table under a pergola covered in wisteria vines, a wooden bench beneath a maple tree now blazing with red and orange leaves, and an intimate firepit area surrounded by Adirondack chairs.

"We host small events out here sometimes," Travis said. "Garden parties, anniversary celebrations, even small weddings. Feel free to take the reins with hosting something for the guests if you'd like," he said with a wink.

At the far end of the garden stood a charming gazebo painted white with green trim to match the inn. Its latticework sides were partially covered with clematis vines.

"The gazebo is a favorite spot for proposals," Kelly said with a smile. "We've had at least two dozen engagements happen right there since we bought the place."

They circled back inside and continued their tour of the inn's rooms. As they walked through each area, Travis and Kelly pointed out all the quirks of the old building—which doors stuck, which window needed extra attention during storms, and where the emergency supplies were kept.

"The inn has fifteen rooms total," Travis said as they climbed the creaking staircase to the second floor. "Each one is different, which guests love, but it also means each one has its own peculiarities."

The grand staircase itself was a work of art, with its curved banister of polished oak and spindles hand-carved with subtle nautical motifs—rope twists, seashells, and waves. The landing featured a spectacular stained glass window depicting a coastal scene with sailboats on the horizon.

"This window is original to the building," Kelly noted as the afternoon sun streamed through the colored glass, casting blue-and-green patterns on the floor. "It survived the big hurricane of 1944 that damaged much of Ocean City."

They walked through several of the guest rooms, each with its own distinct character. The Lighthouse Suite occupied the northwest corner, featuring a circular sitting area built to resemble a lighthouse interior, with panoramic windows offering views of the ocean in the distance.

"This is our most requested room," Travis said. "We're booked solid here through December."

The Maritime Room was decorated with ship models, vintage diving helmets, and framed knot displays. Its bathroom featured an enormous copper soaking tub that gleamed in the afternoon light.

The Garden Room overlooked the back garden and was decorated in soft greens and florals, with a private balcony nestled among the treetops.

The Boardwalk Suite paid homage to Ocean City's famous attraction, with vintage boardwalk photographs, antique carnival game pieces, and even a working vintage penny-arcade game in the corner.

"Each room has its own story," Kelly explained as they continued through the Dunes Room with its subtle palette of sand tones and beach-grass accents. "We've tried to connect them all to some aspect of Ocean City's history or natural environment."

"We have a lot of rooms booked most of the month and have plenty of check-ins tomorrow," Kelly said, handing them a printed guest list. "October is our busiest time in the fall season. People come for the autumn colors and the Halloween festivities, and a lot of them stay for up to two weeks."

Lauren scanned the list, feeling a flutter of anxiety. "That's a lot of names here."

"You'll get the hang of it," Travis assured her. "Most of these are return guests. They know the routine better than we do sometimes."

The Captain's Quarters, located at the top of the house in what was once the attic, featured exposed beams, a king-sized bed built to resemble a ship's berth, and a private cupola with 360-degree views of Ocean City.

"This room is reserved for special occasions," Travis explained. "Anniversaries, honeymoons, milestone birthdays."

The room's sitting area held a collection of antique navigational instruments—spyglasses, compasses, and charts—all displayed under glass. The adjoining bathroom had been modernized with a spectacular rain shower and heated floors while maintaining vintage touches like the claw-foot tub and brass fixtures.

They continued downstairs and into the kitchen, where Kelly walked them through the breakfast routine.

"Doris comes in Wednesdays and Thursdays to help with breakfast prep," she explained. "She's been with us for years and knows this kitchen better than I do. The rest of the staff is pretty flexible. Collin and Gabriel are both in college, studying business. They mainly work evenings when their class schedules allow. Justine works part-time and knows Ocean City like the back of her hand."

"What about laundry?" Lauren asked, thinking of all the bedding for fifteen rooms.

"We have a service for the heavy stuff," Travis answered. "But there's a laundry room in the basement for emergencies and small loads. I'll show you."

The basement tour included the laundry facilities, storage for extra supplies, and the ancient boiler that kept the place warm in winter.

By the time they returned to the main floor, Lauren's head was spinning with information. She glanced at Matt, wondering if he felt as overwhelmed as she did. When their eyes met, he gave her a reassuring smile that made her heart skip a beat, though she noticed the way he kept fidgeting with his watch, a sure sign he was processing a lot too.

"How about we take a break?" Kelly suggested, sensing their information overload. "I've got some limeades for us."

They settled in the parlor, where Travis pulled out a detailed schedule.

"So here's how we're thinking this will work," he said, spreading the papers on the coffee table. "You'll both be working shifts separate from our other employees—a mix of mornings and evenings, depending on the week. We've found it works best to have consistent faces that guests can rely on."

Lauren took a sip of her limeade, the mint and lime helping to clear her head. "And you're sure we can handle this?"

Kelly smiled warmly. "Absolutely. The inn practically runs itself most days. The systems are in place. You just need to be here to welcome guests, solve the occasional problem, and make sure breakfast and afternoon snacks and drinks happen."

"Plus," Travis added, "we'll be available by phone if anything comes up that you can't handle. And Doris knows everything about this place. She's been here since before we bought it."

"When do we start?" Matt asked.

"Tomorrow morning would be perfect," Kelly said.

Lauren felt a surge of panic. She'd never run an inn before. Sure, she had experience with Chipper's and running events, but this was different. What if she messed up? What if the guests complained? What if—

"Don't look so worried," Travis said with a laugh. "Most of our fall and winter guests are pretty laid-back. They're here to relax and enjoy the quieter side of Ocean City in October and the coming months."

"And Binx will help," Kelly added as the cat jumped into Lauren's lap, settling in with a contented purr. "She has a knack for smoothing over any rough patches with guests."

Lauren laughed, but inside, the worry lingered. Running a restaurant was one thing, but preparing breakfast for a house full of guests while managing everything else was another challenge entirely. She glanced at Matt, who gave her a reassuring nod.

* * *

The evening air had grown chilly by the time Matt and Lauren left Starfish Cove Inn. A few stars were already visible in the darkening sky as they walked side by side down the sidewalk, their shadows stretching long beneath the streetlights.

"Well, that was... a lot," Lauren said, pulling her light jacket tighter around her.

Matt nodded. "It's going to be interesting, that's for sure."

"At least we can walk to work," Lauren said. "That's one perk of living in the Gardens neighborhood."

They turned onto Bay Road, the street they both called home. Lauren had been living in her once-dilapidated rental since summer, transforming it through careful renovations into the warm and inviting home she now owned. Matt's place was directly next door, a small but charming bungalow.

"Hey, what's happening at the Stevenson place?" Matt asked, pointing across the street to a house that had been sitting vacant with a For Sale sign for a couple of months. Now the sign was gone, and lights blazed from every window. A large moving truck was parked in the driveway, its back doors wide open.

They slowed their pace, watching as two figures emerged from the house. Even from across the street, they could see that one was tall and lanky with wild, curly hair sticking out in all directions, while the other was shorter with a bright-blue beanie pulled down almost to their eyes despite the mild evening temperature. They wore identical black overalls.

"Well, that's different," Lauren whispered, instinctively lowering her voice though they were too far away to be heard.

The taller figure gestured dramatically toward something inside the truck, arms waving like a symphony conductor. The shorter one simply stood with hands on hips, shaking their head. Then, in perfect unison, both turned to face the street, standing completely still as if surveying their new territory.

"Should we go introduce ourselves?" Lauren wondered aloud.

Before Matt could answer, the taller figure disappeared into the truck and emerged struggling with what appeared to be an enormous telescope on a tripod.

"Careful with Galileo!" the shorter one called out, voice carrying clearly across the quiet street. "We don't want a repeat of what happened in Tucson!"

"Galileo is fine, Dina!" the tall one responded, wobbling slightly as they navigated the telescope down the truck's ramp. "The incident was greatly exaggerated by the authorities."

Matt and Lauren exchanged puzzled glances.

"Did they just say 'authorities'?" Lauren whispered.

"Let's keep walking," Matt suggested quietly.

As they continued toward their homes, trying not to be obvious about watching the strange couple, the pair across the street suddenly turned their heads in perfect synchronization, staring directly at Matt and Lauren with an intensity that made Lauren's skin prickle. Neither waved or called out a greeting; they simply watched.

"Okay, that's a little creepy," Matt murmured.

"More than a little," Lauren agreed.

Through the open front door, Lauren noticed something odd. A series of small, blinking lights moved across the floor of the dimly lit living room. She nudged Matt and nodded toward it.

"What is that?" he asked, squinting to see better.

The lights seemed to be coming from a small circular object that moved with purpose across the floor. It paused at the threshold of the front door then turned in a complete circle before heading back inside.

"A robot vacuum, maybe?" Lauren suggested.

"Probably," Matt said, though he sounded uncertain. "But why is it blinking like that?"

The couple were still watching them, not moving, not speaking. The taller one—Brian, they'd heard—still held the telescope, while the shorter one—Dina—had her hand raised slightly as if frozen in mid-gesture.

"I'm getting weird vibes," Lauren admitted as they reached her driveway.

"You're not the only one," Matt replied, glancing back one more time.

"See you tomorrow?" she asked Matt, eager to get inside.

He nodded. "Bright and early. Ready to be innkeepers extraordinaire."

As Lauren let herself into her house, she couldn't shake the strange feeling that had settled over her. She peeked through her curtains one last time before closing them. The couple were finally moving again, carrying the telescope inside, but something about them continued to unsettle her.

CHAPTER TWO

The morning light bathed Starfish Cove Inn in a warm golden glow as Lauren and Matt arrived, their breath visible in the crisp October air. Matt's hand rested on the small of Lauren's back as they climbed the porch steps, a habit he'd developed since they'd started dating over the summer.

"Think Travis and Kelly will miss this part?" Lauren asked, unlocking the door with a key that still felt foreign in her hand.

Matt chuckled. "The five a.m. wake-up call? Probably not."

Inside, the kitchen awaited them, charming and dated with its butcher-block countertops and copper pots hanging above the island. They quickly fell into their morning routine, preparing a simple breakfast of seasonal pumpkin muffins and apple pancakes. The only hiccup came when Matt accidentally knocked over a freshly brewed carafe of coffee, sending it cascading across the floor. Lauren couldn't help but laugh at his colorful language as he frantically mopped up the mess.

"So much for our professional innkeeper debut," she teased, rescuing his coffee-soaked apron.

By seven thirty, the dining room was ready, with arrangements of russet chrysanthemums, golden marigolds, and deep-burgundy dahlias on each table.

Precisely at eight o'clock, Mrs. Victoria Calloway descended the stairs. Everything about her spoke of meticulous attention to detail, from her perfectly coiffed silver bob to her tweed skirt suit complete with an antique brooch. She surveyed the room with the precision of a building inspector.

"Good morning," she said, her tone implying that whether it was actually good remained to be determined. "You must be the new seasonal innkeepers."

"Yes," Lauren said, extending her hand. "I'm Lauren. And this is Matt."

Mrs. Calloway's handshake was formal and efficient. "Victoria Calloway. Fifteen years I've been coming to Starfish Cove every October."

"It's a pleasure to meet you," Matt said. "Kelly and Travis mentioned you're a regular guest."

"Indeed." Mrs. Calloway's gaze traveled around the room, cataloging every detail. "I always sit at the table in the corner with the view of both the garden and the street."

As Lauren escorted her to her preferred table, Mrs. Calloway continued her assessment. "I noticed the porch swing is hanging unevenly. The left chain is approximately half an inch longer than the right."

Matt blinked in surprise. "I didn't notice that."

"Few do," Mrs. Calloway replied with a hint of satisfaction. "But it creates an imbalance in the sitting experience. Travis and Kelly always ensured it was perfectly level."

As Lauren poured Mrs. Calloway's coffee—black, no sugar—the older woman cast a critical eye at the chalkboard menu. "The menu has changed. Kelly always served blueberry scones on Wednesdays."

"We've incorporated some seasonal ingredients," Lauren explained. "The pumpkin muffins are fresh from the oven."

Mrs. Calloway's expression remained neutral. "I see. I'm quite curious to see what other... innovations you young people have planned."

Before Lauren could respond, the front door chimed. Matt excused himself to greet the new arrivals while Lauren retreated to the kitchen, steadying her nerves.

"Keep calm," she muttered to herself. "She's just one guest. A very observant, particular guest who's been coming here for years and is set in her ways."

When she returned to the dining room, she found Matt chatting with an unusual couple. The woman had vibrant-red hair styled in an asymmetrical cut that defied gravity, and the man sported a full beard and round glasses that gave him an owlish appearance. They wore matching vintage-style utility vests with numerous pockets, each containing what appeared to be different types of small electronic devices.

"Lauren." Matt called her over. "Meet Lori and Jason Hayes. They're checking in for their stay. They're here for the fall foliage and to research local folklore."

"Local folklore?" Lauren asked, her interest piqued.

"Jason's writing a book," Lori explained, tucking a strand of hair behind her ear.

"We've been traveling up and down the coast," Jason added, adjusting his glasses. "Researching local stories. The history in these old buildings is fascinating."

"What brings you to Starfish Cove specifically?" Matt asked.

Lori and Jason exchanged a meaningful look.

"Let's just say we've heard some interesting things about this place," Lori said with a mysterious smile. "We're hoping for some inspiration while we're here."

Matt noticed the bulging pockets on their vests. "What's all that gear you're carrying?"

"Just some research tools we use," Jason explained vaguely, patting one of his many vest pockets. "Most old buildings have their quirks."

"Well, we hope you enjoy your stay," Matt said. "Let me

show you to your room, and then you can join us for breakfast if you'd like."

"Perfect." Lori smiled. "We're famished after the drive, but we'd love to drop off our bags first."

As Matt led the couple upstairs to their room, Lauren spotted Binx, the inn's resident black cat with amber eyes, slinking along the baseboards of the dining room. She smiled at the sight of the mysterious female feline she'd met yesterday. Binx had already shown her talent for appearing and disappearing at will, and Lauren wondered what the guests would make of the enigmatic cat.

Matt returned moments later with Mr. and Mrs. Hayes in tow, and they immediately gravitated toward a table by the fireplace.

As Lauren was about to take their breakfast order, another figure appeared in the doorway—an elderly man with a corduroy cap and an impressive camera that looked more like scientific equipment than photography gear. He peered in with childlike excitement.

"Hello," Lauren greeted him. "Can I help you?"

"Yes, yes," the man said with an enthusiastic Midwestern accent. "George Pemberton. I believe I have a reservation."

Lauren checked the guest book. "Mr. Pemberton, welcome. We weren't expecting you until this afternoon."

"Ah, the early light called to me," he explained, patting his camera lovingly. "October mornings at the Jersey shore—absolutely magical! The light has qualities you simply can't find back in Ohio. Golden but with a crispness. Magnificent for capturing the soul of a place."

"How wonderful." Lauren smiled. "We're serving breakfast now if you'd like to join, and we can get you checked in afterward."

"Perfect." Mr. Pemberton beamed, following Lauren to a table. As they passed Mrs. Calloway, the older woman gave the enthusiastic photographer a look of cool assessment.

"Good morning," Mr. Pemberton said with a cheerful nod to Mrs. Calloway. "Magnificent morning light we're having, wouldn't you say?"

Mrs. Calloway offered him a polite but disinterested nod in return. "I prefer the light in the afternoons, personally." She returned her attention to her coffee with the air of someone who considered the conversation concluded.

Mr. Pemberton, undeterred by her coolness, smiled broadly. "Different perspectives—that's what makes photography so fascinating! Back in Ohio, we don't get this quality of light with the water reflections."

As Lauren returned to the kitchen to check on the pancakes, the front door chimed again. This time, a woman in her fifties entered, dressed in an outfit that could only be described as woodland chic—a flowing dress in earth tones covered by a handmade knitted shawl with what appeared to be actual leaves and twigs woven into the pattern.

"Blessings of the morning to you," she said to Matt, her voice melodic. "I'm Rosemary Hollander. I believe you're expecting me."

Matt consulted the guest book. "Yes, Ms. Hollander. Welcome to Starfish Cove Inn."

"Please, just Rosemary," she corrected, setting down a suitcase made of what looked like vintage tapestry. "I'm here for the Autumnal Herbalists' Retreat. I'll be needing space in your garden to perform my morning sun salutations and a place to dry my fresh-gathered herbs." She glanced around the lobby. "And which room has the strongest natural energy flows? I need to align my crystals properly."

Matt's expression was one of bemused confusion. "I'm... not sure about the energy flows. But we have a lovely room overlooking the garden that gets wonderful morning light."

"That should suffice." Rosemary nodded then suddenly froze, her eyes widening. "Oh! This building has such stories to tell!" She closed her eyes and spread her arms as if embracing the air. "So many lives have passed through here. So many emotions imprinted in these walls."

Just then, Binx the cat emerged from behind a potted fern, stretching languidly before sauntering across the lobby. Rosemary's eyes flew open, and she gasped with delight.

"A familiar!" she exclaimed, kneeling down with outstretched fingers. "Come here, wise one. Share your secrets with me."

To everyone's surprise, Binx approached Rosemary and allowed her to stroke her glossy fur. The cat then stood on her hind legs before placing her front paws on Rosemary's knee as if sharing some feline confidence.

"Oh my," Rosemary whispered, her face alight with wonder. "This is no ordinary cat. She's a guardian of this place." She looked up at Matt with shining eyes. "Did you know your inn has a spiritual protector?"

From her corner table, Mrs. Calloway observed the scene with undisguised skepticism. "I don't recall Travis and Kelly mentioning anything about acquiring a cat," she commented dryly. "Is this a new addition?"

"Yes," Matt explained. "They've only had her for about a month."

"Well"—Mrs. Calloway sniffed—"I hope it doesn't shed on the furniture. Quality upholstery is ruined by pet hair, and I've always appreciated how pristine this inn has been kept."

The Hayes couple had emerged from the dining room, drawn by the commotion. Lori immediately pulled out a small notebook. "A guardian spirit in feline form?" she asked, pen poised. "That fits perfectly with the coastal folklore patterns we've been tracking."

Jason was already fumbling with one of his vest pockets, extracting what looked like a modified thermal camera. "Mind if I take a few readings?" he asked, pointing the device at Binx, who seemed utterly unfazed by the attention.

Before Matt could respond, the door opened again, admitting a tall, thin man in an impeccably tailored suit that seemed at odds with the relaxed atmosphere of the seaside inn. He carried a sleek leather briefcase and surveyed the room with a clinical eye.

"Good morning," he said crisply. "Graham Anderson. I have a reservation."

Matt checked the book again. "Yes, Mr. Anderson. Welcome."

"I'll need a quiet room. Absolute quiet," he said without preamble. "I'm working on my fourteenth mystery novel, and I can't abide distractions."

His professional demeanor cracked slightly as he noticed the gathering around Binx. "What's happening here? Some sort of ritual?"

"The inn's resident cat appears to be holding court," Matt explained with a smile.

"The cat goes wherever it pleases," Mrs. Calloway informed Anderson as he watched the procession. "Though I must say, I'm surprised Travis and Kelly decided to introduce a pet to the inn. In all my years staying here, they've never had animals before."

As the others migrated to the dining room, Lauren slipped back into the kitchen, where she noticed a bookshelf in the corner, half-hidden behind a rolling cart. Curious, she went over to investigate.

The shelves were packed with cookbooks of varying ages, but what caught her eye was a beautiful weathered green one with hand-painted daisies decorating the spine. She pulled it out and opened it carefully. The pages were splattered with coffee stains and cooking remnants, the corners creased from years of use. Handwritten notes filled the margins, with adaptations and observations scribbled next to many of the recipes. At the top of the first page, in elegant script was written "Evelyn Matthews, Innkeeper, 1952."

Lauren turned the pages with reverence, reading the

former innkeeper's notes about which recipes guests preferred and little tricks for making everything from fluffy scrambled eggs to perfect piecrusts. There were notations about seasonal variations and suggestions for adapting recipes based on what was fresh at the local market.

A knock on the doorframe interrupted her reading. Matt stood there, looking both amused and overwhelmed.

"You'll never believe what's happening out there," he said. "The couple working on the book about local legends are asking the mystery novelist about his research process, while Rosemary is trying to convince Mrs. Calloway to try her meditation crystals."

Lauren laughed. "Just a typical day at Starfish Cove Inn, I guess."

"There's something else," Matt said, his expression becoming more serious. "I noticed the porch railing is loose on the east side. Some of the spindles have worked free from the top rail. Should be an easy fix with a drill and some wood glue."

Lauren nodded. "We'll figure it out. One crisis at a time."

Matt glanced at the cookbook in her hands. "What's that?"

"An old cookbook from one of the previous innkeepers," Lauren said, holding it up. "Evelyn Matthews, from 1952. The pages are full of notes and adjustments. This could help us navigate the quirks of this place—and its guests."

"Speaking of which," Matt said with a grin, "you should see the photographer from Ohio. He's set up a tripod in the dining room and is lecturing anyone who'll listen on 'the poetry of morning light on antique woodwork.' Mrs. Calloway looks like she's contemplating using her butter knife for something other than butter."

Lauren peeked through the kitchen door. Mr. Pemberton was indeed photographing the dining room while providing enthusiastic commentary. The Hayes couple had abandoned their breakfast to examine the antique furniture with their various instruments, Rosemary was arranging small crystals on the windowsills, and Graham Anderson was scribbling furiously in his notebook, occasionally glancing up to observe the others. Mrs. Calloway sat with rigid posture, her expression somewhere between disbelief and disdain.

"I overheard the Hayeses talking about setting up some kind of monitoring equipment tonight," Matt whispered. "Something about 'nocturnal energy fluctuations.' And Graham asked me if there were any local unsolved mysteries or if the inn had a colorful history."

"What did you tell him?" Lauren asked.

"I said I didn't know much about the inn's past but a place this old probably has some interesting stories. That seemed to excite him." Matt grinned. "I think our guests are going to keep things interesting."

"And we need to fix that railing before someone gets hurt," Lauren added. Then, glancing over to make sure Mrs. Calloway was out of earshot, she muttered, "Though I wouldn't mind if Mrs. Calloway fell into a rosebush."

Matt laughed. "You don't mean that."

"No, I don't." Lauren sighed. "But I do wonder how Travis and Kelly managed her for fifteen years."

"Maybe there's a secret in that cookbook," Matt suggested. "A special recipe that mellows out difficult guests."

"If there is, I'll make a double batch," Lauren promised.

As they moved back into the dining room, Lauren noticed Mrs. Calloway examining one of the paintings on the wall with critical attention.

"The frame is slightly crooked," she commented to no one in particular. "About three degrees to the left. Travis always made sure the artwork was perfectly level."

Before Lauren could respond, Rosemary approached with a small ceramic pot. "You simply must try my special herbal blend," she said to Mrs. Calloway. "It's excellent for maintaining proper balance in one's energy field."

Mrs. Calloway's eyebrows rose nearly to her hairline. "Is that so?"

Lauren and Matt exchanged glances. Around them, the dining room had transformed into a stage for their guests' eccentricities.

"We did it," Matt whispered, taking her hand for a brief moment. His thumb brushed gently across her knuckles, a familiar gesture that still sent a small flutter through her chest. For just a moment, the chaos around them faded into the background. "First morning survived."

"And it's only nine a.m.," Lauren replied with a laugh. "I can't wait to see what the rest of the day brings."

* * *

The antique grandfather clock in the inn's foyer chimed five times as Lauren checked the guest book one final time. Their first shift as innkeepers was officially coming to a close. She glanced over at Matt, who was arranging a fresh stack of local-attraction brochures on the front desk.

"Ready to call it a day?" she asked, closing the leather-bound book with a satisfying *thud* just as she noticed Justine, another inn employee, coming up the sidewalk out front for her shift.

Matt nodded, stretching his arms overhead. "More than ready. I think my customer-service smile is permanently stuck on my face."

The front door had barely stopped swinging behind them when Matt let out a dramatic sigh. "I never knew managing breakfast could be such an Olympic event. I'm exhausted."

"In a good way, though?" Lauren asked as they fell into step beside each other on the sidewalk.

"Definitely," Matt confirmed. "I think we handled Mrs. Calloway pretty well, though I'm still not sure if she's going to complain about the muffins in her review."

Matt chuckled. "At least the Hayes couple seemed to be enjoying themselves. I caught Jason taking measurements of the staircase banister with some kind of electronic gadget."

"Rosemary was in the garden for two hours, identifying plants and muttering about their 'energetic properties,'" Lauren added with a laugh. "And Mr. Pemberton took at least three hundred photos of the breakfast room."

"Not a bad first day, considering," Matt said, nudging her shoulder gently with his. "It'll make for a good story someday."

As they reached their neighborhood, Lauren stopped short, her mouth falling open. Their new neighbors had completely transformed their front yard overnight.

A full living room set—complete with a floral-patterned sofa, two mismatched armchairs, and a coffee table—was arranged neatly on the lawn. A floor lamp stood beside the sofa, its cord running across the grass and disappearing into an open window. Next to the sofa, the enormous telescope they'd spotted yesterday stood on its tripod, aimed at the afternoon sky.

Brian lounged across the sofa, one leg dangling over the armrest as he enthusiastically conducted an invisible orchestra with a teaspoon. Dina sat cross-legged on the chair, sorting what looked like hundreds of colorful buttons into neat piles.

"Oh my..." Lauren whispered. "Our new neighbors just got even weirder."

From somewhere inside the house, Mozart's *Symphony No. 40* blasted at a volume that seemed to make the windows vibrate. Those windows, Lauren noticed, were now draped with a series of clashing neon curtains in colors of pink, green, and orange.

"Did they move in yesterday and already set up... whatever this is?" Matt asked, gesturing vaguely at the lawn living room.

As Matt and Lauren approached, Brian spotted them and jumped up from the sofa.

"Dina! The neighbors!" he called out excitedly. "The ones with the symmetrical walking patterns!"

Dina looked up from her button sorting and waved enthusiastically. "Hello! Do you like our outdoor entertainment space? Brian thinks it's revolutionary. I think it's going to rain tomorrow and he's going to regret this whole thing."

"It is not going to rain tomorrow. I've checked seventeen different weather apps," Brian said, appearing slightly annoyed.

"And I checked the clouds," Dina countered, pointing skyward. "Those are definitely pre-rain-formation patterns."

Lauren couldn't help herself. "So… you put your living room on the lawn?"

"Indoor-outdoor living integration!" Brian declared as if it were the most obvious thing in the world. "Why should furniture be constrained by walls and ceilings?"

"He read about it in a magazine from 2021," Dina stage-whispered, rolling her eyes affectionately. "Now we're 'revolutionizing suburban-living paradigms.'"

"Plus," Brian added, patting the telescope affectionately, "Galileo here needs an optimal viewing position. Can't exactly set him up in the living room, can we?"

"Galileo?" Matt asked, eyeing the large telescope.

"Our pride and joy," Dina explained, standing up to adjust the telescope slightly. "We've mapped fourteen previously undocumented celestial anomalies with this beauty."

"Although, after the Tucson incident…" Brian began then stopped abruptly.

Both neighbors suddenly went quiet and exchanged a look.

"The Tucson incident was greatly exaggerated," they said simultaneously then burst out laughing.

"Would you care to join us this evening?" Brian asked, gesturing to the empty armchairs. "We're celebrating successful relocation day!"

"With tea!" Dina added, holding up a mug that read

World's Okayest Sister. "Though I can't guarantee what kind it is. Brian labeled all our kitchen boxes in his own invented coding system."

"It seemed more efficient at the time," Brian defended, adjusting the telescope slightly. "Much more precise language."

"He forgot his own system halfway through," Dina confided to Lauren. "So now we have no idea what's in any of the boxes."

At that moment, a small robotic vacuum cleaner with blinking lights emerged from the house, made its way down the porch steps with a series of concerning thumps, and began methodically vacuuming the lawn.

"Your vacuum cleaner is…" Lauren pointed.

"Oh, that's Sparky," Brian said fondly. "He's confused. The move has been hard on him."

"We're still looking for his charging station," Dina added. "It's in one of the mystery boxes, along with all of my left shoes."

Matt chuckled. "Moving is always chaotic."

"We'll, um, have to take a rain check," Lauren said, trying not to stare at the vacuum cleaner now attempting to climb a tree. "Had a long day at the inn."

"Next time!" Brian nodded enthusiastically.

Matt and Lauren said goodbye and continued walking.

"That was…" Lauren began as they reached her porch.

"Yeah," Matt agreed with a laugh. "It really was."

"Want to come in for a cup of tea that isn't labeled in indecipherable code?" Lauren asked, fishing her house key from her pocket.

"Sounds perfect," Matt replied, glancing back at their bizarre neighbors. "Though I'm not sure any tea could compete with whatever 'indoor-outdoor living integration' experience we just witnessed."

CHAPTER THREE

Lauren adjusted a garland of autumn leaves along the banister at Starfish Cove Inn. The salt-tinged breeze slipped through a partially open window, carrying with it the distant sound of waves and the earthy fragrance of fallen leaves. She stepped back to admire her handiwork, pleased with how the rustic oranges and deep reds complemented the polished wood of the grand staircase.

"What do you think?" she called down to Matt, who was untangling a string of miniature pumpkin lights near the reception desk.

"Looks great," he replied, glancing up from his own decorating struggles. "Very... autumnal."

Lauren descended the stairs, careful not to disturb her arrangement. "I found three more boxes of decorations in the storage room."

"Speaking of which," Matt said, finally freeing the last knot in the lights, "I've got the pumpkin bread in the oven. The whole place should smell like cinnamon and nutmeg in about twenty minutes."

As if on cue, Binx appeared at the top of the stairs, her black tail swishing with interest as she surveyed Lauren's decorating efforts. The cat made her way down, carefully stepping between the leaves and ribbons on the banister.

"I think she approves," Lauren said with a smile.

The front door chimed, and Lauren turned to see two new guests enter. The couple looked to be in their late twenties, both dressed in coordinating outfits that screamed old money—she in a camel cashmere sweater over a collared shirt, he in a navy quarter-zip with khaki pants. Their matching boat shoes completed the prep school alumni look.

"Hello," Lauren greeted them, moving toward the reception desk. "Welcome to Starfish Cove Inn."

"Hi there," the woman replied with a polite smile. "I'm Chloe Whitfield, and this is my husband, Parker. We have a reservation for two weeks."

Matt joined Lauren at the desk, checking the leather-bound ledger. "Whitfield… Yes, here you are. You'll be in the Maritime Room." He looked up with a smile. "Did you have a good drive in?"

"It was fine, thank you," Parker said, his voice carrying a slight Boston accent. His eyes darted around the lobby, taking in the vintage furnishings and fall decorations. "This place is as charming as the website promised."

"We're so glad you think so," Lauren said, retrieving their room key from the wooden key cabinet behind the desk. "Let me show you to your room, and then you can join us for some refreshments in the parlor if you'd like. We're putting out some afternoon tea and cookies shortly."

As Lauren led the couple up the stairs, Parker commented on the building's age. Before showing them to the Maritime Room, Lauren briefly explained it was built in 1912 and converted to an inn in the 1930s. The couple seemed impressed by the nautical theme and especially the copper soaking tub in the bathroom.

As Lauren turned to leave, Chloe caught her arm gently.

"This is exactly why we chose this inn," Chloe said, settling onto the edge of the bed. "We wanted something with character for our anniversary vacation. Somewhere peaceful and quiet."

"Well, you'll certainly find that here," Lauren assured them. "Ocean City is lovely in October—all the beauty but none of the summer crowds."

"Perfect," Parker said, giving his wife a warm smile. "We're looking forward to a relaxing stay."

When Lauren returned to the lobby, she found Matt arranging pumpkin-shaped cookies on a tiered tray. Another tray of mugs of hot apple cider sat ready nearby.

"The Whitfields seem nice," she commented, grabbing a cookie from the tray. "They are very appreciative of the inn's character."

"Good to hear," Matt replied, slapping her hand playfully as she reached for a second cookie. "These are for the guests."

"I'm quality testing," Lauren protested with a grin. "It's part of my innkeeper duties."

Matt rolled his eyes but couldn't suppress a smile. "Fine. One more, but that's it. Can you help me carry the cider out to the porch? I think Mr. Pemberton is already out there with his camera."

Lauren took another cookie, savoring the spicy sweetness. "Sure. I bet he's documenting the 'magnificent October light' or something equally poetic."

Together, they gathered the trays and made their way toward the porch, where guests were beginning to gather. Lauren balanced the cider carefully, inhaling the warm, cinnamon-laced steam that rose from the mugs.

After they'd set everything up for the guests, Matt headed back toward the kitchen. "I'm going to grab the pumpkin bread out of the oven. It's just about done."

Lauren nodded and slipped away to the library, wanting to see if there might be any books about the inn's history. The room was empty save for Binx, who was curled up in one of the leather armchairs, sound asleep.

Lauren scanned the bookshelves, eventually finding a slim volume titled *Historic Ocean City: A Pictorial Journey*. She pulled it from the shelf and settled into the chair opposite Binx, who opened one eye to acknowledge her presence before returning to her nap.

She flipped through the pages until she found a section on historic buildings. There, among photographs of the boardwalk and old hotels, was an old image of Starfish Cove Inn from what appeared to be the 1920s. The caption read, "Originally built as a summer home for Philadelphia industrialist Edward Matthews in 1912, this Queen Anne-style house was converted to an inn in 1937 by his daughter, Evelyn, following his mysterious disappearance during a storm in 1935."

Lauren read the passage again. Mysterious disappearance? That certainly sounded like the foundation for a ghost story. She continued reading, learning that the inn had operated continuously since 1937, passing through several owners before Travis and Kelly purchased it years ago.

A soft creaking sound made her look up. Jason and Lori Hayes stood in the doorway, their expressions brightening when they spotted the book in Lauren's hands.

"Finding some interesting reading material?" Jason asked, adjusting his round glasses.

"Just learning a bit about the inn's history," Lauren replied.

The couple exchanged excited glances and moved farther into the room. Lori perched on the arm of a nearby chair while Jason remained standing, his hands thrust deep into the pockets of his utility vest.

"Anything particularly fascinating?" Lori asked, trying and failing to sound casual.

Lauren hesitated then decided there was no harm in sharing what she'd just learned. "Apparently, the original owner disappeared during a storm in 1935. His daughter converted the house into an inn afterward."

"Disappeared, you say?" Jason leaned forward eagerly. "No body ever found?"

"The book doesn't say," Lauren admitted. "Just that it was mysterious."

"Interesting historical context," Lori said, pulling out her ever-present notebook. "We're always looking for places with rich local histories. Have you noticed anything unusual since you started working here?"

Lauren shook her head. "We just started yesterday. Everything's been perfectly normal, aside from juggling the various guest preferences."

"That's what makes it so intriguing," Jason said, his eyes gleaming behind his glasses. "The best hauntings are the ones that fly under the radar. Not commercialized or exploited."

"I wouldn't put too much stock in local legends," a new voice commented from the doorway. Graham Anderson stood there, his tall frame filling the entrance. "As someone who writes mystery novels for a living, I can tell you that most so-called hauntings have perfectly rational explanations."

"Ah, the skeptic arrives," Jason said good-naturedly.

"Not a skeptic," Graham corrected, stepping into the library. "Just someone who prefers evidence over speculation. Old houses make noises. That's a fact of physics and materials science, not the supernatural."

Lori tucked her notebook away, eyeing Graham with interest. "You write mysteries, Mr. Anderson. Surely you appreciate the value of a good enigma."

"I appreciate them in fiction," he replied crisply. "Reality is a different matter."

The conversation was interrupted by the arrival of Rosemary, who drifted into the library with an armful of what appeared to be fresh herbs.

"I sense a disturbance in the energy of this room," she

announced, sniffing the air delicately. "You're discussing the resident spirits, aren't you?"

Lauren couldn't help but notice how the atmosphere in the room shifted immediately. Jason and Lori straightened, their attention fully captured. Even Graham, despite his proclaimed skepticism, turned toward Rosemary with apparent interest.

"So you've noticed something too?" Lori asked eagerly.

Rosemary nodded solemnly. "This place is alive with impressions from the past. Not all buildings retain memories like this one does." She looked directly at Lauren. "You must have felt it by now."

Put on the spot, Lauren wasn't sure how to respond. She certainly hadn't experienced anything supernatural, but she also didn't want to disappoint Rosemary or the others.

"I haven't been here long enough to notice anything unusual," she said diplomatically.

"The spirits reveal themselves in their own time," Rosemary replied with an enigmatic smile. "And only to those who are receptive."

Graham made a small noise that might have been a suppressed snort of disbelief.

"You doubt the existence of energies beyond our understanding, Mr. Anderson?" Rosemary challenged.

"I doubt interpretations that leap to the supernatural when mundane explanations would suffice," he replied evenly.

Before the discussion could escalate further, Matt appeared in the doorway, the tray in his hands laden with steaming mugs and a plate of thickly sliced pumpkin bread.

"Afternoon refreshments," he announced. "Who's hungry?"

As the group congregated around the refreshments, Lauren noticed Parker and Chloe Whitfield hovering uncertainly in the hallway. She waved them in.

"Perfect timing," she called to them. "We were just about to enjoy some freshly baked pumpkin bread."

The Whitfields entered cautiously, their eyes darting

around the room as if expecting to see something lurking in the corners.

"We were just discussing the history of the inn," Lauren said, hoping to draw them into normal conversation.

"What a beautiful inn," Chloe remarked, accepting a mug of cider from Matt. "We're so happy we chose to stay here."

As everyone settled in with their refreshments, Parker suddenly cleared his throat. "I don't mean to put a damper on things," he began hesitantly, "but did anyone else experience anything... unusual a little while ago?"

The room fell silent. Lauren noticed Jason and Lori exchange a quick, excited glance.

"Unusual how?" Lauren asked carefully.

Chloe looked embarrassed. "It's probably nothing, but we heard some strange sounds in our room. Like footsteps in the hallway, except no one was there when Parker checked."

"And there was this cold spot," Parker added, his voice lowering. "Right in the middle of our room. Even with the heat on."

"Not only that," Chloe continued, her eyes wide, "but the bathroom door closed by itself while we were unpacking. No draft, no windows open. It just... shut."

Jason had already pulled out one of his mysterious devices from his vest pocket, his expression alight with excitement. "That's fascinating! Would you mind if we took some readings in your room? For our research?"

"Research?" Chloe asked, looking confused.

"The Hayeses are here studying local folklore," Lauren explained quickly.

"We'd be grateful for any explanation," Parker said, seeming relieved that someone was taking their concerns seriously. "It was... unsettling."

Graham rolled his eyes. "Professional ghost hunters? Is that what you call yourselves?"

"We prefer 'paranormal researchers,'" Lori corrected.

"I think it's all rather exciting," Rosemary chimed in, helping herself to a mug of cider from Matt's tray. "A house with history should have a few spectral residents."

Mrs. Calloway, who had been observing the conversation from her seat by the window, finally spoke up. "In all my fifteen years staying at this inn, I've never encountered anything supernatural," she stated. "Though I will say the third step on the back staircase has always creaked in a rather peculiar manner." She took a deliberate sip of her tea. "Travis always said it was the wood expanding, but it does sound remarkably like someone sighing."

The room fell silent as everyone processed this unexpected contribution from the usually critical Mrs. Calloway. Jason looked like he was about to pounce on this new information, but Graham spoke first.

"Precisely my point," he said, nodding at Mrs. Calloway. "Natural explanations for supposedly supernatural phenomena."

As the conversation devolved into a spirited debate about the existence of ghosts, Lauren caught Matt's eye across the room.

He gave her a small shrug and a smile that said, "What have we gotten ourselves into?"

* * *

Later that evening, after most of the guests had retired to their rooms, Lauren and Matt sat at the kitchen island, sharing the remains of the pumpkin bread.

"So," Matt said, breaking off a piece. "Are we running a haunted inn now?"

Lauren laughed softly. "According to the Hayes couple, we might be. I did some research this afternoon after the Whitfields mentioned their strange experiences. The original owner, Edward Matthews, disappeared during a nor'easter in 1935.

According to local legend, he went down to secure his boat during the storm and was never seen again."

"That's sad but not necessarily supernatural," Matt pointed out.

"True, but there's more. When his daughter, Evelyn, converted the house to an inn two years later, guests reported seeing a man in old-fashioned clothes walking the hallways at night, leaving puddles of seawater behind him."

"Okay, that's creepier," Matt admitted. "But still, old houses, creaky floors, overactive imaginations…"

Lauren took a sip of her tea. "The stories persisted. In the 1950s, a guest claimed to have been woken by a soaking-wet man standing at the foot of her bed, asking if anyone had found his boat. In the 1970s, the innkeepers at the time reported lights turning on and off by themselves, especially during storms."

"Where did you find all this?" Matt asked.

"The local historical society has a website with a section on local legends," Lauren replied. "There were a few old newspaper clippings too. Apparently, a local paper did a Halloween feature on 'haunted' local buildings in 1989, and Starfish Cove Inn made the list."

"So it's been part of local folklore for decades," Matt mused. "I wonder why Travis and Kelly never mentioned it."

"Maybe they didn't know? Or maybe they didn't want to scare us off," Lauren suggested, echoing Matt's earlier theory. "Though I have to say, the Hayes couple seem absolutely thrilled by the possibility."

"Not to mention the Whitfields, who seem genuinely freaked out by their experience," Matt added.

"And Rosemary with all her talk of energies and impressions."

"Even Graham seemed interested, for all his skepticism," Matt observed.

They sat in comfortable silence for a moment, the only sound the gentle ticking of the antique clock on the wall.

"You know," Lauren said finally, "even if we don't believe in ghosts, this could actually be good for business. People love this kind of thing, especially around Halloween."

Matt raised an eyebrow. "Are you suggesting we lean into the haunted-inn angle?"

"Maybe a little." Lauren grinned. "Nothing dishonest, but we could put out some of the more atmospheric decorations I found in those boxes. There's a whole set of vintage candelabras and some really beautiful old lanterns."

"And I could make those cinnamon cookies cut into ghost shapes that I saw in Evelyn's cookbook," Matt added, warming to the idea.

"Exactly! Embrace the season and the history without explicitly claiming the place is haunted."

Matt nodded slowly. "I could get behind that. But what about when guests like the Whitfields ask about their experiences?"

"We tell them the truth—that the inn has a rich history and there have been stories over the years, but we personally haven't experienced anything unusual," Lauren suggested. "Let them draw their own conclusions."

"Sounds like a plan," Matt agreed. "Though I have to admit, this place is pretty creepy sometimes. All those creaking floorboards and drafty corners."

As if to emphasize his point, a sudden gust of wind rattled the kitchen windows, making them both jump.

Lauren laughed nervously. "Maybe we should head out. Collin and Gabriel are here to take over, though I'm guessing they're in the basement taking care of some laundry," she said, glancing around.

They cleaned up their small midnight snack and switched off the kitchen lights. As they walked to the front door together, Lauren couldn't help glancing over her shoulder at the darkened corners of the inn, the stories she'd read swirling in her mind.

"You don't actually believe in ghosts, do you?" Matt asked quietly as they stepped onto the porch.

"No," Lauren replied quickly. Then, after a pause, she said, "But if I did, I'd say Edward Matthews sounds like a relatively friendly spirit. Just a man looking for his lost boat."

Matt grinned. "Well, maybe he can help us find a solution for keeping Mrs. Calloway happy."

"I'll stop by your place after I shower and change," Lauren said, zipping up her jacket against the autumn chill. "We can figure out dinner then."

"Sounds good," Matt replied. "Maybe I'll make that pasta dish you liked last week."

As they separated to walk to their neighboring homes, Lauren couldn't help thinking about Evelyn Matthews, who had transformed her family home into an inn after losing her father. Lauren wondered what kind of woman she had been, to channel her grief into creating a place where travelers could find comfort and rest. The cookbook Lauren had found suggested someone who cared about details, who wanted her guests to feel at home.

Later, after a relaxing dinner at Matt's place—his promised pasta with gorgonzola sauce and a bottle of red wine they'd picked up on their last trip to a local vineyard—Lauren found herself back in her own cottage, her mind still spinning with thoughts of the inn and its possible ghostly resident.

Matt had remained practical through dinner, suggesting logical explanations for the Whitfields' experiences and drafting a to-do list for checking the heating system and any spots where drafts might create cold pockets of air. But he'd also seemed intrigued, especially when Lauren shared more details from her research. They'd spent over an hour brainstorming Autumn-themed breakfast ideas and planning how to decorate the inn for the season.

In her house, Lauren opened the window slightly to let in the cool October air. The gentle lapping of bay water and the occasional call of night herons drifted in, along with the scent of salt marsh. She climbed into bed, pulling the quilt up to her chin, suddenly very aware of every creak and groan of her cottage.

"No such thing as ghosts," she whispered to herself as she turned out the light. Yet she couldn't help adding, "But if you're out there, Mr. Matthews, we'll take good care of your house. I promise."

Outside her window, the wind picked up, rustling the leaves of the old maple tree in the darkness. For just a moment, it almost sounded like a reply.

CHAPTER FOUR

Lauren's first sip of coffee hadn't even hit her system when she stepped onto her cottage porch and heard her neighbor's cheerful voice.

"Morning, Lauren!" called Erin from the neighboring property. "Come on over and finish that coffee with me. John's already left for his fishing trip, and I've made my chocolate croissants."

Lauren smiled, grateful for the invitation. After the interesting day at the inn yesterday, a quiet moment with her neighbor was exactly what she needed.

"You don't have to ask me twice," she called back, making her way across her yard to Erin's porch, where colorful chrysanthemums framed the steps.

"You look tired," Erin observed as Lauren settled into one of the cushioned wicker chairs. "Is the inn keeping you busy?"

Lauren accepted a warm chocolate croissant with gratitude. "You have no idea. We've had quite the cast of characters check in this week."

Erin chuckled. "Sounds like you've got your hands full. The characters you meet when working with the public never cease to amaze me."

Lauren took a bite of the croissant, closing her eyes briefly in appreciation. "These are amazing, Erin."

"Family recipe," Erin said with a wink. "Have you met those peculiar new neighbors across the street yet? The ones who moved in recently?"

Lauren laughed. "Brian and Dina? Oh yes. They're beyond eccentric. Matt and I watched them setting up their entire living room on the front lawn yesterday—sofa, chairs, even a floor lamp plugged in through a window. It was basically an open-air living space."

"So that's what that was!" Erin exclaimed. "I saw all that furniture but didn't get close enough to investigate. I thought maybe they were having some kind of yard sale."

"Definitely not a yard sale," Lauren said, shaking her head. "Brian kept going on about 'revolutionizing suburban-living paradigms' like he'd invented something groundbreaking. And they have a robot vacuum cleaner they've named Sparky that wanders around trying to vacuum the grass. The poor thing kept getting stuck trying to climb a tree."

Erin's eyes widened. "A vacuum on the lawn? I thought I was hallucinating when I saw something mechanical bumping into their tree yesterday!"

"Oh, it's real," Lauren confirmed. "Brian treats it like a pet. Told us 'the move has been hard on Sparky' like it has feelings. They're the strangest people I've ever met."

Erin leaned forward, her voice dropping conspiratorially. "Well, I've been watching them from my porch at night, and they get even stranger after dark."

"I can only imagine," Lauren said, genuinely curious. "What have you seen?"

"Two nights ago, around three in the morning, they moved in a full-sized carousel horse. Not a little one—an actual amusement park–sized carousel horse with poles and everything. It took both of them to carry it, and they were arguing about the best placement for 'optimal energy absorption' or something like that."

"That actually makes sense for them," Lauren said, wide-eyed. "Their entire house is like a carnival crossed with a laboratory."

"And last night? They set up a ping-pong table in the driveway and played for an hour, wearing what looked like hazmat suits and headlamps."

"Of course they did," Lauren said dryly. "Totally normal midnight ping-pong attire."

"Normal ping-pong doesn't involve stopping every few minutes to adjust the table with spirit levels and protractors," Erin continued. "They were measuring angles and distances like it was some kind of scientific experiment rather than a game."

Lauren nearly choked on her croissant. "That doesn't surprise me at all. When we met them, Brian mentioned something about a 'Tucson incident' before Dina cut him off. They both went quiet and then said it was 'greatly exaggerated.' I'm starting to wonder what that was about."

"And their house lights!" Erin added. "They were blinking on and off in some kind of pattern for almost an hour straight. Not random, mind you. It seemed intentional, like some kind of code. John was convinced they were trying to communicate with... something."

"You know what's even stranger?" Erin continued, lowering her voice further. "I talked to Gladys at the real estate office yesterday, and she told me the house was sold to a couple named Jill and Dean Moffet. But they introduced themselves to you as Brian and Dina."

Lauren's eyes widened. "That is odd. Though given everything else about them, using different names seems like the least unusual thing they're doing.

"Something doesn't add up with those two," Erin said, shaking her head. "I'd keep an eye on them if I were you."

* * *

That afternoon, Lauren was reviewing the breakfast menu when the front door of Starfish Cove Inn burst open, bringing with it a flurry of excited voices and the scent of expensive perfume.

"Hello? Is anyone here? We've arrived for the Starling-Francis wedding!"

Lauren exchanged a confused glance with Matt, who had been polishing the antique silverware at the dining room table. They both moved toward the lobby, where they found five women in coordinating pastel outfits, surrounded by designer luggage and garment bags.

"Welcome to Starfish Cove Inn," Lauren said, trying to hide her confusion. "I'm Lauren, and this is Matt. We're the innkeepers."

A tall woman with sleek blond hair stepped forward, hand extended. "I'm Vanessa Starling, mother of the bride. We spoke with Travis about all the arrangements for this weekend's wedding." Her smile was warm, but her eyes were scanning the lobby, clearly taking inventory.

Matt glanced at Lauren before answering. "I'm afraid Travis and Kelly didn't mention any special arrangements to us. They left us in charge but—"

"Didn't mention?" Vanessa's perfectly sculpted eyebrows shot up. "But we've been planning this for months! We're staying here for the wedding weekend. Travis promised our rooms would be ready."

"Mom, relax," said one of the younger women, stepping forward. She had the same elegant features as Vanessa but with a gentler expression. "I'm Emma, the bride. We're here for the weekend. The ceremony and reception are at Seaside Gardens, but Travis promised us the five best rooms for our stay."

"We have all the details in the email confirmations," another woman said, pulling out her phone.

Lauren's mind raced. They would need to shuffle things around to accommodate five additional guests who were clearly expecting premium treatment. Finding rooms with the best views on such short notice would require some creative problem-solving.

"Why don't we all move to the parlor?" she suggested, trying to keep her voice steady. "I'll make some tea while we sort this out."

As the women followed her, Lauren caught Matt's eye and mouthed, "Call Travis!"

While Lauren settled the wedding party in the parlor, Matt retreated to the kitchen, phone in hand. After what seemed like an eternity, he returned, his expression a mixture of relief and anxiety.

"Okay, so Travis confirmed the booking," he whispered to Lauren as she arranged a tray of hastily assembled refreshments. "Apparently, it was in a separate events calendar they forgot to mention to us. He's emailing over all the details right now."

Lauren took a deep breath and carried the tray to the parlor, where the women were in the midst of an animated discussion about their dresses.

"So, good news," she announced with a brightness she didn't feel. "We've confirmed your booking. There was just a small communication mix-up during the handover. Matt and I will do everything we can to make sure your stay is perfect."

Vanessa looked skeptical. "Travis assured us he'd personally ensure our rooms would have the best views and be prepared with the special amenities we requested."

"Mom, please." Emma sighed. "I'm sure Lauren and Matt will do fine." She turned to Lauren with a kind smile. "We've brought some welcome bags for our other guests who are staying elsewhere. Could we perhaps keep those here until the wedding? And is there a space where I could do a final fitting of my dress tomorrow?"

Lauren's event experience kicked in, and she found herself nodding confidently. "We can absolutely handle that. Let's get you settled in your rooms first, and then we can find the perfect space for your fitting."

As Lauren led the bride and her party upstairs to their rooms, she passed Matt in the hallway, who was staring at his phone with a look of horror.

"Travis just sent the full list of requirements," he whispered. "It's... extensive."

"We'll figure it out," Lauren assured him, though her own confidence was wavering. "Just keep the other guests happy while I handle the wedding party."

Over the next few hours, Lauren immersed herself in wedding preparations, listening to detailed descriptions of the bride's requests and making notes of all their needs for the weekend. Emma, despite her mother's high-strung energy, turned out to be refreshingly down-to-earth.

"I know this is a lot to throw at you," she confided as they walked through the inn, checking out the rooms. "My mother tends to... escalate things. I wanted something simple, but..." She gestured to the numerous bags her bridesmaids were unpacking, filled with personalized robes, gift baskets, and what appeared to be custom slippers for each guest.

"It's going to be beautiful," Lauren assured her. "We'll make sure your stay here is perfect before your big day."

While Lauren managed the wedding party, Matt found himself juggling the inn's regular guests and their growing concerns about the sudden influx of activity.

"Mr. Anderson," Matt said, knocking gently on the mystery writer's door. "I wanted to let you know there will be additional guests checking in today. They're here for a wedding this weekend. We'll try to keep the noise to a minimum, but I wanted to give you a heads-up."

The door opened a crack, revealing Graham's stern face. "I specifically requested a quiet environment for my writing. Do you know how difficult it is to capture the perfect atmosphere for a murder scene with bridesmaids giggling in the background?"

"I understand completely," Matt said, thinking quickly. "Which is why I wanted to offer you our private study off the library. It has a solid oak door and is quite soundproof. You'd have it entirely to yourself this weekend."

Graham considered this, his expression softening slightly. "Well, that's... actually quite thoughtful. Thank you."

One by one, Matt visited each guest, addressing their concerns and finding creative solutions. For Mr. Pemberton, he suggested a special opportunity to photograph the "authentic human emotion" of a bride before her wedding day. For Rosemary, he ensured her crystals wouldn't be disturbed by the wedding party. And for the Hayes couple, he arranged private access to the historic boathouse for their research, well away from the wedding preparations.

"Did you know," Matt mentioned casually to Jason, "many historic inns like this one have traditional rooms where brides stay before their weddings? It's part of the local history."

Only Mrs. Calloway remained unmoved by Matt's diplomacy. "This is completely unacceptable," she declared as Matt explained the situation over afternoon tea. "I have stayed here every October for fifteen years, and never once has my peace been disturbed by wedding parties."

Matt refilled her teacup with the precision she preferred—exactly three-quarters full. "I completely understand your feelings, Mrs. Calloway. Which is why I wanted to personally assure you that we've arranged for the wedding party to use the east wing rooms, farthest from yours. And I've personally spoken to them about quiet hours."

Mrs. Calloway sniffed. "I suppose that's something, at least."

By late afternoon, Lauren had found spaces for all the wedding party's belongings, set up a small sitting room where

Emma could have her dress fitting the next day, and created a schedule that would allow the wedding party to enjoy the inn without disrupting the other guests.

"You've been amazing," Emma told Lauren as they finished arranging the welcome bags for the off-site guests. "I honestly thought this was going to be a disaster when Mom realized Travis wasn't here, but you've handled everything beautifully."

"We're happy to help," Lauren replied, genuinely pleased with their efforts. She glanced across the hall, where Matt was helping the bridesmaids with their luggage, his manner confident and reassuring.

As dinnertime approached, the wedding party prepared to leave for their rehearsal dinner at Seaside Gardens. Lauren and Matt stood at the front door, waving them off.

"We'll probably be back late," Vanessa warned as she climbed into the waiting car. "The dinner is scheduled until ten, and then the girls want to have some champagne back here."

"No problem," Matt assured her with a smile that only Lauren could tell was slightly strained. "We'll leave the porch lights on for you."

With the wedding party gone, the inn settled into a temporary calm. Lauren and Matt took advantage of the quiet to regroup in the kitchen.

"Crisis averted, for now," Lauren said, leaning against the counter.

"Until they come back from the rehearsal dinner," Matt replied with a tired smile. "But at least we have a few hours of peace."

"We did pretty well, didn't we?" Lauren observed. "Getting everyone situated and keeping the other guests relatively happy."

"We make a good team," Matt said simply. "Though I'm not sure I'd want to manage a wedding party every weekend."

"Well, it's certainly a crash course in inn keeping," Lauren said. "Dealing with the unexpected and all that."

They spent the next couple of hours preparing for the following day's breakfast and making sure everything was in order for the wedding party's late return.

Just after eleven, the relative quiet of the inn was shattered by the sound of car doors slamming, followed by high-pitched laughter and excited chatter. The wedding party had returned, and from the sound of it, the rehearsal dinner had been a success, with perhaps a bit too much champagne.

"Shh! There are other people sleeping!" one voice attempted to whisper, though it was still clearly audible through the closed front door.

"It's not even midnight!" another replied, followed by more laughter.

Matt and Lauren exchanged glances as they hurried to the lobby to greet the returning group.

"Welcome back," Lauren said quietly as she opened the door. "How was the rehearsal dinner?"

"It was fabulous!" Emma exclaimed, her cheeks flushed with excitement. "The wedding is going to be perfect!"

"Ladies," Matt interjected gently, "we do have other guests who might be sleeping. Maybe we could keep the volume down a bit?"

"Of course, of course." Vanessa nodded, though her stage whisper wasn't much quieter than her regular voice. "Girls, let's be considerate."

As the group moved through the lobby and toward the stairs, a door on the second floor opened, and Graham Anderson's annoyed face appeared over the railing.

"Some of us are trying to work," he called down, his voice tight with irritation.

"So sorry!" Emma called back, which only seemed to annoy the writer further.

He retreated with a disgruntled huff, slamming his door.

"I'm so sorry about that," Lauren said after returning to the kitchen, where Matt was preparing a quick snack for the wedding party. "I don't think Mr. Anderson is going to be writing any happy endings tonight."

"At least Mrs. Calloway's room is on the other side of the inn," Matt replied. "Though I wouldn't be surprised if she's already drafting a formal complaint."

It took another hour to get the wedding party settled. The bridesmaids wanted ice for their champagne, then extra pillows, then instructions on how to work the antique ceiling fan. Vanessa couldn't get her room's window to close properly, and Emma suddenly remembered she needed a steamer for her veil in the morning.

Finally, around midnight, the inn fell quiet. Lauren and Matt found themselves outside, gathering empty glasses that the wedding party had left on the porch and in the garden before heading inside.

"What a day." Lauren sighed, sinking onto one of the wooden benches. The October night was clear and cool, with stars scattered across the dark sky. "I thought we'd handled everything when they left for the rehearsal dinner. I didn't expect the midnight party."

Matt sat beside her, close enough that their shoulders touched. "It could have been worse. At least they're all tucked in now. And they'll be out at the wedding venue most of tomorrow."

"True," Lauren agreed. "And we managed to keep most of the other guests happy, despite the disruption."

They sat in comfortable silence for a moment, listening to the rhythmic sound of waves in the distance and the gentle rustling of leaves in the garden.

"You know," Matt said after a while, "despite all the chaos, I'm enjoying this. Working with you, solving problems, figuring things out as we go."

Lauren smiled in the darkness. "Me too. We do make a

good team."

"Remember yesterday when the Hayeses were going on about those strange noises they heard?" Matt asked. "And how the Whitfields claimed their bathroom door closed by itself?"

"And Rosemary with all her talk about 'energies' and 'impressions'?" Lauren added with a quiet laugh.

Matt leaned back, gazing up at the stars. "You know, with all these ghost stories floating around about this place, I keep catching myself listening for strange noises. Earlier today, I was in the attic looking for extra blankets, and I heard this creaking sound that made the hair on the back of my neck stand up."

"What was it?" Lauren asked.

"Just the wind, I think. But for a second..." He trailed off with a self-conscious laugh. "I guess this place is getting to me too."

Lauren nudged his shoulder. "Don't tell me you're starting to believe in Edward Matthews and his ghostly search for his lost boat."

"No, no," Matt protested with a smile she could barely see in the darkness. "But you have to admit, this old place has a certain... atmosphere. Especially at night. I wonder what the Hayeses would say if they saw us now, sitting in the dark garden, talking about the inn being haunted," Matt mused.

"They'd probably start an investigation immediately," Lauren replied, picturing Jason with his various gadgets. "I can just imagine—"

Her words were cut short by a loud *thump* from somewhere inside the inn, followed by what sounded like footsteps crossing the upstairs hallway. They both froze, listening intently.

"That's probably just one of the wedding party," Matt whispered, though he didn't sound convinced.

Another *thump* sounded and then what sounded distinctly like a door opening and closing. Lauren glanced at Matt, whose face was barely visible in the dim light from the porch.

"Should we go check?" she asked, already rising from the bench.

Matt nodded, and they made their way quietly back into the inn. The lobby was empty and still with only the gentle ticking of the grandfather clock breaking the silence. They crept up the stairs, careful to avoid the steps that creaked.

The upstairs hallway was empty, all doors closed. Lauren and Matt exchanged puzzled glances.

"Maybe it was just the old house settling," Lauren suggested, not entirely convinced.

As if in response, a cold draft suddenly swept through the hallway, causing the wall sconces to flicker. From somewhere down the hall came what sounded like a soft sigh.

Lauren felt goose bumps rise on her arms as she grabbed Matt's sleeve. "Did you hear that?"

Before Matt could answer, the door to an unoccupied room slowly swung open with a long, drawn-out *creak*. They stood frozen, staring at the empty room now revealed before them.

"Drafts," Matt said firmly, though his voice had an edge to it. "Old houses have drafts."

"Exactly," Lauren agreed quickly. "The ocean winds cause pressure changes. It's perfectly normal."

Neither of them moved toward the door.

"We should probably close it," Matt finally said, taking a hesitant step forward.

Just as he reached for the doorknob, a sudden *thump* came from inside the room as if something heavy had fallen. Matt jerked back, bumping into Lauren.

"What was that?" she whispered.

They peered cautiously into the darkened room. Nothing seemed out of place. The bed was neatly made, the curtains drawn against the night. Another soft *thump* came and then what sounded like footsteps crossing the room toward them.

Lauren and Matt stumbled backward, nearly tripping over each other. The footsteps stopped at the threshold of the door.

"There's nothing there," Matt said, his voice higher than usual. "Just the house settling."

Lauren nodded vigorously. "Absolutely. Old floorboards. Happens all the time."

They turned to head back downstairs, walking slightly faster than normal. Behind them, the door to the room closed with a decisive *click*.

Neither looked back.

CHAPTER FIVE

The afternoon sky over Starfish Cove Inn had transformed from the brilliant blue of morning to a worrying slate gray. Lauren stood at the parlor window, watching as dark clouds gathered on the horizon, their edges tinged with an ominous yellowish glow. The weather had been perfect for Emma's wedding earlier in the day, but now, nature seemed determined to end the celebrations with a dramatic flourish.

"That doesn't look good," Matt commented, coming to stand beside her. He was holding his phone, his brow furrowed in concern.

"What's the forecast saying?" Lauren asked, though the answer was written across the darkening sky.

"Coastal storm. It's going to hit us tonight," Matt replied, scrolling through the weather alert. "Strong winds, heavy rain, possible flooding in low-lying areas. They're predicting power outages throughout Ocean City."

Lauren sighed. "Of course. Just when we thought we had everything under control."

They'd spent the morning helping Emma prepare for her wedding, steaming her veil and ensuring the bridesmaids had everything they needed before they departed for Seaside Gardens. The ceremony had gone off without a hitch, according to Vanessa's enthusiastic text messages, complete with photos of Emma looking radiant in her gown. Now the wedding party was at the reception, blissfully unaware of the weather that awaited their return.

"We should start preparing," Lauren said. "If the power goes out, we need to be ready."

Matt nodded. "I'll check all the window latches and bring in anything from the porch and garden that might blow away. We should find all of the flashlights and batteries too."

"I'll inventory our food situation and make sure we have enough that doesn't require cooking," Lauren added. "And I'll fill some containers with water, just in case."

As they separated to tackle their respective tasks, the wind outside began to pick up, sending fallen leaves skittering across the porch in swirling patterns. Lauren could hear the distant sound of wind chimes from a neighboring property, their once-melodic tinkling now frantic.

In the kitchen, Lauren found Binx perched on the windowsill, watching the gathering storm. The cat's tail swished back and forth with agitation.

"You feel it, too, huh?" Lauren said, pausing to scratch behind the cat's ears. Binx leaned into Lauren's touch but kept her gaze on the window as if watching for something only she could see.

After taking stock of their supplies, Lauren was relieved to find they were reasonably well-prepared. The pantry contained crackers, jars of peanut butter and jelly, and some canned goods. There was plenty of fresh fruit that would need to be consumed quickly if the power went out, and thankfully, the refrigerator was stocked with cheese, cold cuts, and vegetables.

As Lauren worked, Mrs. Calloway appeared in the kitchen doorway, her silver bob as perfectly styled as ever despite the humidity.

"I've experienced two major coastal storms during my October stays," she announced without preamble. "The worst was in 2012, when the power was out for three days. Travis and Kelly served hot tea and sandwiches by the fireplace." Her tone made it clear she expected similar service regardless of the circumstances.

"We're preparing for the possibility of power loss," Lauren assured her. "Is there anything specific you need, Mrs. Calloway?"

"My chamomile tea," the older woman replied. "With exactly half a teaspoon of honey. And perhaps some extra blankets. The northwest corner room tends to get drafty during storms."

"I'll bring those up shortly," Lauren promised.

"See that you do," Mrs. Calloway said with a brisk nod before turning to leave. At the doorway, she paused. "And do be careful with the candlesticks from the dining room if you need to use them. They're sterling silver and require a specific polish that Travis always kept in the utility closet."

After Mrs. Calloway departed, Lauren continued her preparations, filling several pitchers with water. She located all the candles in the inn—from elegant tapers to practical tea lights—and set them out strategically throughout the main rooms, making sure matches were nearby.

She could hear Matt moving furniture on the porch, the scrape of chair legs against wood punctuated by the increasing howl of the wind. Through the window, she watched as he secured the porch swing, wrapping its chains more tightly to prevent it from banging against the house.

By early evening, most of the guests had returned to the inn, seeking shelter from the worsening weather. The Hayes couple arrived soaking wet from their excursion to the nearby jetty, their electronic equipment carefully wrapped in plastic bags. Rosemary returned from a hot yoga session, her face still glowing with exertion beneath her rain-spattered shawl.

Mr. Pemberton rushed in with his camera equipment, lamenting the loss of the "extraordinary natural compositions" he had been trying to capture at Corson's Inlet.

The Whitfields appeared from their walk downtown, laughing as they shook rain from their hair, their cheeks flushed from hurrying through the first sprinkles.

Only Graham Anderson had remained in the inn all day, emerging from the study just long enough to inquire about the weather before retreating again with a fresh pot of coffee.

Matt finished securing the exterior just as the rain began, drumming against the roof and windows with increasing intensity. He came inside, his hair damp and shirt clinging to his shoulders. Lauren felt her breath catch slightly as she watched him run a hand through his wet hair.

"Everything's as ready as it can be," he reported, accepting the towel Lauren offered. "I moved all the porch furniture against the wall and tied it down. The garden shed is locked, and I closed all the shutters on the vulnerable windows."

Lauren handed him a mug of hot coffee. "The guests are all accounted for except the wedding party. Vanessa texted to say they're still at the reception but planning to leave by midnight."

"In this weather?" Matt glanced toward the window, where rain was now streaming down in sheets. "They might be better off staying put."

"I told her that, but she insisted they'd be back. Apparently, the venue is concerned about flooding in their parking lot and wants everyone out before it gets worse."

As evening fell, the storm intensified. The wind howled around the corners of the old building, finding every gap and crevice to whistle through. The rain pounded against the windows with such force it sounded like handfuls of pebbles being thrown. The large oak tree outside the library window swayed ominously, its branches scraping against the glass.

Matt and Lauren had just finished setting out a simple

spread of cheese, crackers, fresh fruit, and tea sandwiches in the dining room when the first flash of lightning illuminated the sky, followed seconds later by a crack of thunder that seemed to shake the very foundation of the inn.

"That was close," Matt said, moving to the window.

As if in response, the lights flickered once, twice, and then plunged the inn into darkness.

"And there it goes." Lauren sighed. She fumbled in her pocket for her phone and switched on its flashlight. "Time for plan B."

They worked quickly in the dim light, lighting candles and distributing flashlights to the guests who had gathered in the dining room. Lauren was grateful for the inn's many fireplaces as Matt set about building a fire in the main parlor, its warm glow soon creating a cozy atmosphere despite the chaos of the storm outside.

"Well, this is certainly atmospheric," Rosemary commented, settling into an armchair near the fire, her collection of crystals arranged on a small table beside her. "Perfect for connecting with the elemental energies."

"I've got my equipment running on battery power," Jason Hayes announced, setting up what looked like a modified monitor on the coffee table. "If there's any paranormal activity, storms like this tend to amplify it. The electromagnetic fluctuations create ideal conditions."

"Nonsense," Graham Anderson muttered, though he sat close enough to observe Jason's equipment with poorly disguised interest. "It's just ionization in the atmosphere creating static electricity."

"Whatever it is, it's good material for my next book," Jason replied good-naturedly.

The Whitfields had claimed one of the love seats, Parker's arm around Chloe's shoulders as she jumped at each crack of thunder. "Think of it as an adventure," he murmured to her, though his own expression suggested he was less than thrilled with the situation.

Mr. Pemberton seemed the most delighted of all, setting up his tripod in the corner of the room. "The play of candlelight on these antique furnishings is spectacular!" he exclaimed, adjusting his camera settings.

Only Mrs. Calloway remained unimpressed, perched on the edge of her chair with perfect posture, sipping her tea and occasionally checking her watch as if the storm were an inconvenience that had failed to respect her schedule.

"This reminds me of those hurricane parties we used to have back home," Chloe offered, warming to the situation. "Everyone gathering together, sharing stories while the storm rages outside."

"What a charming tradition," Rosemary said with a smile. "Communal experiences during nature's fury have been part of human culture since ancient times. Many believe such moments thin the veil between worlds."

"There you go again with the supernatural nonsense." Graham sighed, though there was less edge to his voice than usual.

"I think it's nice," Lauren said, distributing blankets among the guests. "All of us gathered together like this. Kind of cozy, despite the circumstances."

Matt returned from checking the upstairs, his flashlight beam preceding him into the room. "Everything looks secure up there. No leaks that I could see." He joined Lauren near the refreshment table they'd set up, lowering his voice. "Any word from the wedding party?"

"Nothing since Vanessa's last text," Lauren replied. "I'm worried about them trying to make it back in this weather."

"Me too." Matt frowned. "But for now, let's focus on keeping everyone here comfortable."

As the storm continued to rage outside, the atmosphere inside gradually transformed from one of anxiety to unexpected camaraderie. Lauren improvised a dessert of fruit and chocolate fondue, using tea lights to keep the chocolate warm.

Matt discovered a collection of vintage board games in the library and brought them out. "Since we're all stuck here anyway," he suggested, "why not pass the time with some games?"

"Excellent idea!" Jason immediately agreed, while Lori set aside her notebook.

"I haven't played board games in years," Mrs. Calloway remarked, though she made no move to leave.

A surprisingly competitive Monopoly match soon developed between Graham and Jason, while Rosemary and Chloe engaged in an intense game of chess by candlelight. Mr. Pemberton acted as self-appointed photographer of the evening, capturing what he called "the extraordinary human connection amid nature's fury."

A particularly violent gust of wind chose that moment to rattle the windows, causing several of the guests to jump.

"Just the wind," Lauren assured everyone, distributing mugs of hot tea. "This old place has weathered worse storms."

"The building has good bones," Mrs. Calloway agreed, unexpectedly supportive. "Constructed properly, unlike so many modern structures."

Before anyone could respond, the front door burst open with a *bang*, sending several people to their feet in alarm. Flashlight beams swung wildly toward the entrance, where a group of rain-soaked figures stood silhouetted against the night.

"Oh my, is everyone having a game night?" Vanessa's voice carried over the howl of the wind as she stepped into the lobby, followed by Emma, her new husband, and the bridesmaids. "In the dark?"

"Mom, it looks amazing in here," Emma said, pushing back her hood to reveal her once-perfect updo now plastered against her head. "Like something out of a storybook."

Matt hurried to close the door against the storm while Lauren went to greet the wedding party.

"We were worried about you," she said, helping Vanessa out of her dripping coat. "The storm is terrible."

"It's been quite the adventure," Vanessa said, her typically commanding tone softened by relief. "The reception venue started flooding, and we had to evacuate. But somehow, walking in to find all of you playing board games by candlelight—it's oddly perfect."

"Well, come in and get warm," Lauren urged, guiding them toward the parlor. "We're all gathered by the fire. There's food and drinks and, as you can see, board games to pass the time."

"I call next game of Monopoly," one of the bridesmaids announced, making her way toward the game table. "I was state champion back in college."

"Oh, you're on," Jason challenged with a grin, making room at the table.

To Lauren's surprise, the wedding party quickly integrated with the other guests, their initial exhaustion from the storm transforming into excitement about the impromptu game night. Emma's new husband, a tall man with a friendly smile, immediately bonded with Graham over their shared knowledge of strategy games, while the bridesmaids clustered around Rosemary, fascinated by her crystal collection that she'd used to mark her place in the chess match.

Lauren found herself standing with Matt near the refreshment table, watching the unexpected mingling with amazement.

"Are you seeing this?" she whispered. "I was dreading a clash of personalities, but they're actually getting along."

"Nothing like a power outage and board games to bring people together," Matt replied with a grin. "Though I can't believe they made it back in this weather. That was dangerous."

A particularly violent gust of wind rattled the windows, followed by a flash of lightning that illuminated the room, briefly showing the stark contrast between the storm's fury outside and the warm cocoon they'd created within. The thunder that followed seemed to rumble through the inn's bones.

As the evening progressed, the storm began to show signs of weakening, though the rain continued to drum steadily against the windows. The guests had settled into a comfortable rhythm, passing board games around and sharing stories of their travels and experiences.

Later, as the guests began to drift upstairs to bed—some in pairs or groups, reluctant to face the dark hallways alone during the storm—Lauren found herself beside Matt in the kitchen, where they were cleaning up the last of the dishes by lantern light.

"You know," she said, drying a mug and setting it on the counter, "I think this might be my favorite night at the inn so far. Despite everything."

Matt nodded, understanding in his eyes. "There's something about a crisis that brings out the best in people. Or at least, brings them together."

"Even Mrs. Calloway seemed to be enjoying herself by the end," Lauren marveled. "I saw her actually laughing at one of Parker's jokes."

"And Vanessa bonding with Rosemary over wedding stress remedies," Matt added with a chuckle. "Who would have predicted that?"

A particularly strong gust of wind moaned through the eaves, causing them both to glance upward.

"This old place is holding up well," Lauren commented, impressed by the sturdy construction that had weathered so many coastal storms over the decades.

"Travis and Kelly chose well when they bought it," Matt agreed, his voice warm in the darkness. "And we're doing a pretty good job taking care of it for them, I think," he said as he moved closer to Lauren, putting his arm around her waist and pulling her in for a tender hug.

As if in answer, the lantern between them flickered briefly, its light dimming for just a moment before burning steady once more. They exchanged glances, and then, by unspoken mutual agreement, decided not to comment on the timing.

CHAPTER SIX

The day after the storm dawned clear and brilliant as if to apologize for the previous night's chaos. Lauren arrived at Starfish Cove Inn early, coffee mug in hand from her morning brew at home. She stood on the porch, watching as workers cleared fallen branches from the street. The air smelled clean and fresh with that particular scent that only follows a major storm—a mixture of wet earth, sea salt, and renewal.

Power had been restored around five in the morning, awakening everyone with a chorus of beeping appliances and suddenly illuminated lamps that had been left on during the outage. Now, as morning sunlight glinted off puddles in the garden, there was little evidence of the tempest that had rattled windows and united strangers just hours before.

"Morning," Matt said, joining her on the porch with his own mug. "How'd you sleep at your place? I kept waking up to check if the power was back."

"Better than I expected," Lauren replied. "Though I kept waking up, thinking I heard thunder."

Matt nodded, leaning against the railing beside her. "Same here. But the guests seem to have weathered it well. Mrs.

Calloway has already informed me that her morning tea was 'acceptable,' which I'm taking as high praise."

Lauren laughed. "The wedding party is still asleep. Emma texted to say they'd probably be down later than usual. I think they're all exhausted from yesterday's excitement."

"Can't blame them," Matt said. "Wedding, evacuation, storm—all in one day."

They stood in comfortable silence for a moment, watching a squirrel navigate a fallen branch that now connected two trees in the garden.

"I've been thinking," Lauren said finally. "Last night was... special, in a way. Seeing everyone come together like that."

"It was," Matt agreed. "Who would have thought board games by candlelight would be such a hit?"

"We should think about ways to create more moments like that," Lauren continued, turning to face him. "Not waiting for a storm, of course, but intentional gatherings. Something unique to Starfish Cove."

Matt's expression brightened with interest. "I like where this is going. What did you have in mind?"

"I'm not sure yet," Lauren admitted. "But last night made me realize there's something powerful about bringing people together in unexpected ways. The Hayeses wouldn't normally interact with Mrs. Calloway or the Whitfields with Rosemary. But somehow, it worked."

"Hmm." Matt considered this, thoughtfully taking a sip of his coffee. "I noticed a storage closet upstairs the other day when I was looking for extra blankets during the storm. Looked like it might have some old records or historical items. Maybe we could find some inspiration there? See what special traditions this place might have had in the past?"

"I love that idea," Lauren said, feeling a flutter of excitement. "We've got some time before breakfast service. Want to start now?"

Thirty minutes later, they found themselves in a cramped,

dusty storage room on the third floor. Boxes of holiday decorations were stacked alongside outdated electronics and unused furniture. A set of antique golf clubs leaned in one corner, while a forgotten mannequin draped in yellowed lace occupied another.

"Looks like no one has organized this room in decades," Matt observed, carefully moving a box labeled X-MAS from atop a wooden trunk.

Lauren sneezed as dust danced in the shaft of sunlight streaming through the small dormer window. "Look at this," she said, pointing to a large trunk with brass corners. "It looks ancient."

Together, they cleared a path to the trunk and knelt beside it. The lid creaked in protest as Matt lifted it, revealing stacks of leather-bound albums, manila folders, and what appeared to be framed photographs wrapped in old bedsheets.

"Jackpot." Lauren breathed, gently lifting out the top album. Its cover was worn leather with the words Starfish Cove embossed in faded-gold lettering.

"Let's take these downstairs," Matt suggested. "I don't think my allergies can handle much more of this dust, and we have about an hour before we need to start on breakfast."

They transported their finds to the library before spreading the contents across one of the reading tables by the fireplace. Lauren had just opened the first album when Matt uncovered something even more intriguing—a box filled with newspaper clippings, some yellowed with age, others more recent, all carefully preserved in plastic sleeves.

"*Ocean City Gazette*, 1937," Matt read from one of the older clippings. "'Matthews Estate Converted to Seaside Inn.' There's a photo here of Evelyn Matthews cutting a ribbon across the front door."

Lauren peered over his shoulder. The monochrome photograph showed a slender woman with dark hair styled in the fashion of the 1930s, scissors poised to cut a ribbon while a small crowd looked on.

"She looks so young," Lauren commented. "The book I found said she converted the house after her father disappeared in 1935. She couldn't have been more than in her early twenties here."

"Brave of her to take on such a venture, especially in that era," Matt said. He carefully turned to another clipping. "Here's one from 1952, 'Starfish Cove Inn Celebrates Fifteen Years.' It mentions that the inn became known for its 'welcoming atmosphere and special community events.'"

"What kind of events?" Lauren asked, interest piqued.

Matt scanned the article. "It doesn't say specifically, just that 'locals and visitors alike gathered regularly for Evelyn's famous seasonal celebrations.'"

They continued exploring, finding photographs spanning decades—the inn decorated for Christmas in the 1940s, a garden party in the 1960s, guests in bell-bottoms lounging on the porch in the 1970s.

"Look at this one," Lauren said, carefully removing a color photograph from one of the albums. It showed a gathering in the inn's dining room, the table extended to its full length and surrounded by people in evening attire, candlelight illuminating their faces. "It's dated 1983. 'Midnight Supper Club, Winter Solstice Gathering.'"

"Midnight Supper Club?" Matt took the photo, studying it. "There's more here." He flipped through several more pages revealing similar gatherings spanning years—different faces, different decorations, but all with the same intimate, celebratory atmosphere.

"Here's an article about it," Lauren said, pulling out a clipping from the *Ocean City Sentinel*. "'Starfish Cove's Midnight Supper Club Becomes Local Tradition.' It says Evelyn Matthews started it during World War II, when food was rationed. People would bring what they could, and she'd transform it into a midnight feast once a month. It became a way for the community to come together during difficult times."

"I wonder when they stopped doing it," Matt mused, flipping through more recent albums.

The answer came in the form of a clipping from 1997. "Sadly, after many years, Starfish Cove Inn's famous Midnight Supper Club tradition has ended," Matt read aloud. "The inn's owners, citing changing times and financial considerations, have discontinued the monthly gatherings that became a hallmark of Ocean City's off-season community life."

"So it ended over a decade before Travis and Kelly even bought the place," Lauren noted, studying the faded newspaper article.

The discovery kept them engrossed until the aroma of burning potatoes jolted them back to the present. They rushed to the kitchen to rescue the breakfast potatoes, just in time to avoid disaster. The morning passed in a blur of serving guests, checking in with those departing, and ensuring rooms were ready for new arrivals.

It wasn't until late afternoon, when the inn settled into its brief quiet period between checkout and check-in, that they were able to return to their discovery. They spread the materials across the library table once more, this time with fresh coffee and the remains of the morning's blueberry muffins to sustain them.

"I can't stop thinking about this Midnight Supper Club," Lauren said, examining a particularly charming photo from what appeared to be the 1970s, showing a table decorated with autumn leaves and candles, surrounded by smiling guests in wide-collared shirts and one woman sporting a feathered hairstyle. "It seems like such a perfect tradition for this place."

"It really does," Matt agreed. "Community, good food, and bringing people together. It aligns perfectly with what we were talking about this morning."

Lauren's eyes lit up. "What if we revived it? Not exactly the same way, of course, but our own version."

"I love that idea," Matt said, his enthusiasm matching hers. "We could do it just during our time here, through the winter months. Special themed dinners, maybe?"

"Yes! And we could incorporate local history, seasonal ingredients..." Lauren trailed off, her mind racing with possibilities. "But wait, we should probably check with Travis and Kelly first. There must have been a reason the tradition stopped."

Matt nodded, reaching for his phone. "Good point. Let's call them now, and we can ask about the ghost stories while we're at it."

He put the call on speaker, and after a few rings, Travis's cheerful voice filled the room. "Matt! Lauren! How are things at the old homestead? You two handling everything okay?"

"We're doing great," Matt replied. "The storm last night was quite an adventure, but everything's intact. No leaks or damage that we can find."

"That's a relief," Travis said. "Those nor'easters can be brutal. Kelly was worried about you guys."

"We managed fine," Lauren assured him. "Actually, we're calling because we found something interesting today. A box of old photos and newspaper clippings in the storage room upstairs. Did you know about the Midnight Supper Club that used to be held here?"

There was a pause on the other end. "Vaguely. The real estate agent mentioned something about it when we bought the place. Some kind of regular dinner gathering, right?"

"It was more than that," Matt explained. "It was a community tradition that ran for around sixty years, from World War II until the late nineties. Monthly midnight suppers that brought together locals and visitors."

"We were thinking about possibly reviving it," Lauren

added. "Not permanently, just during our time here. Would you be okay with that?"

"Sure. Why not?" Travis replied easily. "As long as you don't burn the place down or scare away our regular guests. Sounds like a fun idea, actually."

"There's something else we wanted to ask," Matt continued. "We've had a few guests mention strange experiences—noises, cold spots, that sort of thing. Some of them are convinced the inn is haunted. Do you know anything about that?"

Travis laughed. "Oh, those old ghost stories. Yeah, they've been floating around since we bought the place. Something about the original owner disappearing in a storm. Honestly, it's just an old house. Creaky floors, drafty windows. You know how it is."

In the background, they heard Kelly's voice. "Is that Matt and Lauren? Let me talk to them."

A moment later, Kelly was on the line. "Hi, you two! Travis is filling me in. The Midnight Supper Club sounds like a wonderful idea. I'd love to see that tradition come back."

"What about the ghost stories?" Lauren asked. "Travis thinks it's just the old house settling, but some of our guests seem pretty convinced the inn is haunted."

There was a slight hesitation before Kelly answered. "Well... I don't know about ghosts, exactly. But I will say, there have been times when I've been alone in the inn and heard things that were hard to explain. Footsteps upstairs when no one was there. Items that seemed to move on their own."

"Kelly believes in that stuff," Travis interjected, his voice slightly distant as if he'd moved away from the phone. "I keep telling her it's just the wind, or she forgot where she put things."

"I know what I've heard," Kelly insisted. "And it's not just me. Doris, who's worked there forever, refuses to be alone in the building after dark. She says she's seen a man in old-fashioned clothes walking through walls."

"Through walls?" Matt repeated, raising an eyebrow at Lauren.

"Listen," Kelly continued, her voice lower as if sharing a confidence, "I'm not saying the place is definitely haunted. But there's something... I don't know, something that feels off sometimes. Especially during storms or late at night when the place is quiet. Just a feeling that you're not alone."

"Anyway," Travis cut in, clearly wanting to change the subject, "about this Midnight Supper Club idea. If you want to give it a try, we're all for it. Could be good for business, actually. Give guests a reason to book during the slower months."

They discussed logistics for a few more minutes before ending the call with promises to keep Travis and Kelly updated on any new developments, supernatural or otherwise.

"Well, that was interesting," Matt said as he set his phone down. "Kelly definitely thinks there's something to these ghost stories."

"And Travis definitely doesn't," Lauren added with a smile. "But they're both supportive of the Midnight Supper Club idea. I think we should do it."

"Me too," Matt agreed.

They spent the next hour sketching ideas, drawing inspiration from the historical photos while adding their own modern touches. The picture that emerged was enticing—a candlelit gathering that would honor the inn's past while creating something new and memorable.

As evening approached, they realized they had missed lunch entirely and were now famished. The inn was quiet, with most guests out for dinner, and they had the evening off since Gabriel and Collin were handling the front desk.

"Want to grab something to eat?" Matt asked as they carefully returned the historical materials to their boxes. "I'm starving."

"Definitely," Lauren agreed. "Actually, Erin texted earlier about meeting up at Howie's Creamery for ice cream. I told her maybe, depending on how the day went. She and John are heading there around eight."

"Ice cream for dinner?" Matt grinned. "I'm in."

As they walked the few blocks to the popular ice cream shop, the sun was setting, painting the sky in vivid oranges and pinks that reflected off the water. October in Ocean City had a special quality—the summer crowds gone, the seaside town reclaiming its more intimate character. The boardwalk was quiet but not deserted, with locals and a few off-season visitors enjoying the mild evening.

They spotted Erin and John waiting outside the ice cream shop, the familiar storefront illuminated against the darkening sky.

"There you are!" Erin called, waving them over. She wore a well-loved Ocean City sweatshirt, looking relaxed and casual after a day on the water. John stood beside her, tall and easy-going as ever. "We were worried you might not make it."

"Sorry we're late," Lauren said, greeting her friend with a hug. "We got caught up in some research at the inn."

"Research?" John raised an eyebrow. "Sounds serious."

Matt laughed. "Just digging into the history of the place. We found some interesting old traditions we're thinking about reviving."

They joined the line that stretched outside the shop's door. Despite the offseason, the place remained popular with locals who knew that October meant special seasonal flavors like pumpkin cheesecake and apple cider sorbet.

"So how's the inn-keeping life treating you?" Erin asked as they shuffled forward. "Any horror stories yet?"

Lauren and Matt exchanged amused glances. "Well, we did have a power outage during last night's storm," Lauren said. "And the place was full, including a wedding party."

"That sounds like a nightmare," John commented.

"Actually, it turned out to be kind of magical," Matt replied. "Everyone gathered in the parlor, we played board games by candlelight, and it ended up being this unexpectedly fun evening."

"Oh my," Erin said suddenly, her voice dropping to a whisper. She nudged Lauren sharply. "Don't look now, but weird-neighbors alert. Three o'clock."

Despite the warning, Lauren couldn't help glancing in the indicated direction. Sure enough, there were the new neighbors, Brian and Dina, standing near the front of the line.

As the four of them watched discreetly, Brian and Dina reached the counter and placed what appeared to be an extraordinarily large order. The teenage server behind the register looked increasingly bewildered as the list grew.

"Are they seriously ordering seven different sundaes?" Erin whispered incredulously. "There are only two of them!"

"Maybe they're getting some to go," Matt suggested. "Or picking up for friends?"

Their question was answered moments later when Brian and Dina collected their order—seven elaborately constructed sundaes arranged on a large tray—and proceeded to a corner table. No one else joined them. Instead, they positioned the sundaes between them and began an odd ritual, each taking a single bite from one sundae before moving methodically to the next.

"What in the world?" Lauren breathed, watching the peculiar dessert choreography unfold.

The line moved forward, bringing them closer to Brian and Dina's table. Lauren tensed, hoping they wouldn't be noticed. The last thing she wanted was another awkward encounter with her odd new neighbors.

As they inched closer, snippets of Brian and Dina's conversation became audible. They were speaking to someone seated at the next table—a middle-aged man in a polo shirt who seemed to be enduring rather than enjoying their attention.

"...absolutely vital to maintain the correct balance," Dina was saying, her voice carrying clearly above the shop's background noise. "Most people don't understand the importance of precise consumption patterns."

"It's not just about taste," Brian added solemnly. "It's about the chemical composition and how it affects the receptors."

The man nodded vaguely, looking as if he regretted his choice of seating.

"We've been developing this method for years," Dina continued, gesturing with her spoon. "You can't imagine the difference it makes in cognitive functioning."

"That's... interesting," the man replied, clearly searching for an escape route.

Erin leaned close to Lauren's ear. "What are they talking about? It sounds like they think ice cream is some kind of brain medicine."

Before Lauren could respond, it was their turn to order. They quickly selected their flavors—pumpkin cheesecake for Lauren, mint chocolate chip for Matt, cookie dough for Erin, and a coffee milkshake for John—and retreated to the farthest available table, safely out of Brian and Dina's line of sight.

"That was close," Lauren said, settling into her chair. "I really didn't want to have to make small talk with them."

"What was that about 'precise consumption patterns'?" John asked, stirring his milkshake. "They made eating ice cream sound like a scientific experiment."

"They're definitely odd," Matt agreed. "But harmlessly so, I guess. Just eccentric neighbors with strange ice cream habits."

Erin wasn't convinced. "I don't know. Something about them seems... off. And I'm not just talking about their sundae-sampling technique." She lowered her voice again. "Did you hear what Brian said to that guy as we were paying? Something about 'the procedure being nearly perfected' and how they were 'close to a breakthrough.'"

"Maybe they're scientists," Matt suggested. "Or working on some kind of food research project."

"In a house like that with no visible means of support?" Erin shook her head. "I've only lived next door to them for less than a week, and I've already noticed they don't seem to have regular jobs, but they're always coming and going at odd hours, carrying strange items."

By the time the four finished their ice cream, Brian and Dina had departed, leaving behind seven meticulously sampled sundaes, each with only a few bites taken from it.

As they walked back to their homes through the quiet streets, Lauren couldn't help but reflect on the encounter. "Do you think we should be concerned about Brian and Dina?" she asked Matt as they turned onto their street. "Erin seemed genuinely unsettled by them."

Matt considered this. "They're definitely unusual, but I don't get any dangerous vibes from them. Just... eccentric. Every beach town has its characters, right?"

"I suppose," Lauren agreed. "Something definitely feels off, though."

CHAPTER SEVEN

"Ready for a proper autumn adventure?" Matt asked with a grin as he drove across the Ninth Street Bridge, leaving Ocean City behind. The car windows were cracked to let in the cool fall air as they crossed over the sparkling bay waters. "Apple picking, pumpkin patches—the whole October experience."

Lauren smiled, watching a cluster of seagulls drift and circle against the bright-blue sky. "Absolutely."

Fall had settled over Ocean City and the surrounding Jersey Shore, painting the landscape in rich amber and crimson. Beyond the bridge, they passed the wetlands displaying golden-brown reeds, and occasional maple trees flamed with colors of red, orange, and yellow.

Matt reached across the console briefly as he changed gears. "I've mapped out a classic autumn day for us," he said, his eyes on the road. "We'll start with this farm I discovered last year that has a bit of everything—pumpkins, apples, and some great local cider."

Twenty minutes later, Matt turned onto a gravel road lined with split-rail fencing. As they crested a small hill, a sprawling farm came into view with various fall attractions spread across the property. A hand-painted sign announced Robinson's Family Farm.

"This place has everything," Lauren said, taking in the scene. Several families were scattered throughout the grounds, some examining pumpkins while others headed toward apple trees in the distance.

The farm's parking area was only half full, a benefit of visiting on a weekday, and the afternoon had drawn just enough visitors to create a cheerful atmosphere without crowds. As they approached the entrance, the aroma of apple cider and cinnamon hung in the air.

They wandered between rows of pumpkins, some still attached to withering vines, others displayed on hay bales. Lauren approached the selection with the seriousness of an art curator, examining each candidate with careful scrutiny.

"Too lopsided," she declared, moving past an irregularly-shaped pumpkin.

"That's what makes it interesting," Matt protested.

They spent the next half hour selecting their perfect pumpkins —Lauren's a classically proportioned specimen with an impressive stem, Matt's a slightly misshapen one with what he insisted was "character." As they carried their finds back toward the farm stand to pay, the sound of laughter drew their attention.

"The hayride to the apple orchard is about to leave," Matt noted, nodding toward a tractor hitched to a wagon filled with hay bales. "Want to add apple picking to our agenda after we pay and load these into the car?"

"Is that even a question? Of course we do!"

Eventually, they joined the small group boarding the hayride, finding spots on the hay bales that served as makeshift seats. The tractor engine rumbled to life, and they began a gentle journey through the property.

"Perfect weather for this," Lauren commented as the wagon bumped along the path. The October landscape unfolded around them—fields of harvested corn, distant woods blazing with color, and the apple orchard waiting ahead.

The orchard welcomed them with rows of trees laden with varieties of apples—Honeycrisp, Gala, Jonagold, and more. Each guest received a small basket and instructions to pick only the ripe fruit.

They filled their baskets with a variety of apples, discussing potential recipes and comparing the different varieties. When they had collected enough, they headed toward the farm stand, where the aroma of baked goods drew them to a small café area.

"Two ciders and a half-dozen doughnuts," Matt ordered at the counter.

They found a table overlooking the farm's activities. Lauren took her first bite of a doughnut and nodded approvingly. The outside was crisp with cinnamon sugar, the inside warm and cake-like with the subtle tang of apple cider.

"Good call," she admitted, savoring the taste. "Perfect fall food."

After finishing their snack, they browsed the farm store, selecting several varieties of local jam and a jug of fresh apple cider to take home.

Eventually, they made their way back to Ocean City, where Matt parked near the quieter northern end of the boardwalk. A few hearty souls walked the wooden planks, bundled against the ocean breeze.

They strolled along the boardwalk, observing the shuttered amusements and seasonal decorations. Halloween displays filled the windows of the few year-round shops—paper skeletons, fake cobwebs, and carved pumpkins creating a festive atmosphere despite the off-season quiet.

"Ocean City has such a different personality this time of the year," Lauren commented as they paused to watch waves crashing against the shore.

"It's like the town can finally exhale after summer," Matt agreed.

Lauren nodded, pushing herself closer to Matt for warmth as a gust of salty wind swept across the boardwalk. "I love seeing it this way."

They continued their stroll, passing the occasional jogger. A lot of boardwalk shops were mostly shuttered for the season, metal grates pulled down over storefronts that just weeks ago had been bustling with summer tourists.

"Want to head over to Asbury?" Matt suggested. "More places will be open there."

"Good call," Lauren agreed. "I could use some warmth, and I'd love to see what's still open downtown."

They made their way down one of the wooden ramps leading off the boardwalk and walked the few blocks to Asbury Avenue, Ocean City's main shopping district. Unlike the boardwalk, Asbury Avenue maintained much of its vitality year-round, with many shops remaining open to serve the permanent residents.

As they turned onto the avenue, Lauren appreciated how the town had decorated for the season. Lampposts were adorned with autumn wreaths and cornstalks, while storefront windows featured pumpkins, scarecrows, and Halloween displays.

"Oh, let's stop in here," Lauren said, pointing to a whimsical-looking store. "I love this soap shop."

They entered and were enveloped in a symphony of scents —citrus, sandalwood, and the ever-present undertone of sea salt that seemed to infuse everything in Ocean City.

"Welcome!" called a woman arranging a display of bath bombs. "Just let me know if you need help finding anything."

Lauren gravitated toward a display of seasonal bar soaps before picking up a square labeled Harvest Moon and inhaling deeply. The rich scent of pumpkin and spice filled her senses.

"This is amazing," she said, offering it to Matt.

He took a tentative sniff. "Not bad, actually. Usually, these scented things are too much for me, but that's subtle."

Lauren explored the rest of the seasonal collection, picking up soaps labeled Autumn Orchard, Cranberry Cider, and Maple Forest.

"I can't decide," she admitted after several minutes of deliberation.

"The seasonal sampler has all four fall scents in mini bars," the shopkeeper suggested. "Perfect if you want to try them all."

"Sold," Lauren said with a smile, carrying her selection to the counter.

Back on Asbury Avenue, they continued their exploration, stopping in a boutique where Lauren admired a display of chunky sweaters and scarves.

"This would look great on you," Matt said, holding up a deep-burgundy cardigan with wooden buttons.

Lauren checked the price tag and winced slightly but tried it on anyway. The soft wool felt luxurious, and the color complemented her complexion perfectly. "It does look good," she admitted, examining her reflection. "But I probably shouldn't…"

"Consider it a celebratory gift for our new venture as innkeepers," Matt insisted.

Lauren hesitated only briefly before giving in. "Okay, but this means I'm treating for lunch."

After purchasing the sweater, which Lauren immediately wore over her lightweight blouse, they continued down Asbury, window shopping and enjoying the relaxed pace of the offseason.

"Getting hungry?" Matt asked as they approached a simple storefront with a large hoagie painted on the window.

Lauren read the sign. "Sack O' Subs?"

Inside, the sandwich shop was warm and unpretentious, with a handful of small tables and a long counter where orders were placed. The menu board listed dozens of combinations, and the air was fragrant with the smell of fresh bread and grilling meat.

"What's good?" Lauren asked, studying the options.

"Everything, honestly," Matt replied. "But I think their chicken cheesesteak is pretty legendary. And their roast beef and cheese is a classic."

"Perfect. You get one, I'll get the other, and we'll share."

"Deal."

They placed their order—a chicken cheesesteak for Matt and a roast beef and cheese for Lauren—and found a small table by the window while they waited.

"Food should be ready in about five minutes," Matt said, returning from the counter with two sodas. "They make everything fresh."

When their number was called, Matt retrieved the sandwiches, which were wrapped in white butcher paper and served in brown paper bags—simple but appetizing.

Lauren took her first bite of the chicken cheesesteak and closed her eyes appreciatively. The meat was tender and flavorful, the cheese perfectly melted, and the bread had just the right balance of softness and chew.

"This is incredible," she admitted after swallowing. "I see why it's legendary."

They traded halves midway through the meal, and Lauren found the roast beef equally impressive—thinly sliced, perfectly seasoned, and with just enough cheese to complement without overwhelming the meat.

After lunch, they headed back on Asbury Avenue, this time heading south to explore a different section they hadn't visited earlier.

As they strolled, Lauren noticed a storefront with large windows displaying colorful paintings of beach scenes, lighthouses, and seascapes.

"Coastal Wonders Gallery," she read from the elegant sign. "Let's look."

Inside, the gallery was bright and airy, with white walls providing a clean backdrop for the vibrant paintings. Each piece captured some aspect of coastal life—the particular quality of light over the ocean at sunrise, the texture of sand dunes rippled by wind, the architectural details of beach houses.

"These are beautiful," Lauren commented, studying a painting of waves crashing against a jetty.

"Thank you" came a voice from the back of the gallery. A woman in her forties emerged from a small office, wiping paint-stained hands on a cloth. She had brown hair worn up in a casual bun, laugh lines around her eyes, and an easy smile. "I just finished that one last week."

"You're the artist?" Lauren asked, impressed.

"For better or worse," the woman replied with a self-deprecating laugh. "I'm Maddie. This is my gallery."

"The work is incredible," Matt said. "You really capture the light here."

"That's the challenge and the joy of painting this place." Maddie nodded. "The light changes everything." As Maddie moved closer to discuss the painting, she suddenly stopped, her eyes widening slightly as she looked at Lauren.

"I'm sorry, but you look so familiar," she said, tilting her head. "Have we met before?"

Lauren smiled politely, used to such questions since returning to Ocean City. "I spent summers here as a kid, but I've been away for years. Just moved back recently."

"Lauren?" Maddie asked tentatively.

Lauren blinked in surprise. "Yes, that's me. Do we know each other?"

Maddie's face broke into a wide grin. "It's Maddie Scott. My parents had the house next to your grandparents' place on Ocean Avenue! We used to spend all day at the beach together!"

Lauren's jaw dropped as recognition dawned. "Maddie?

You're kidding! I can't believe it's you!" She looked at her old friend with new eyes, seeing past the mature woman to the girl she'd once known. "It's been, what, twenty-five years?"

"At least." Maddie laughed. "The last summer I remember was when we were sixteen and spent most of our time scoping out that lifeguard on Sixth Street."

Lauren grinned, memories flooding back. "Todd! With the bleached hair! We were shameless."

Matt observed their reunion with an amused smile, enjoying the unexpected connection between the two women.

"We were inseparable every summer from when we were about eight until we were teenagers," Lauren explained to Matt.

"We did everything together," Maddie added. "Building sandcastles, miniature golf at Pirate's Cove, riding the Ferris wheel, laying out trying to get tan…"

"I can't believe you recognized me after all these years," Lauren said, still amazed.

"Your smile hasn't changed a bit," Maddie replied warmly. "Plus, I have a good memory for faces. Comes with being an artist, I suppose."

"And look at you now! This is your gallery? These are all your paintings?"

Maddie nodded, gesturing around the space. "Opened two years ago. Best decision I ever made, after the divorce."

"Divorce?" Lauren echoed.

"Yeah, three years ago now. When we split, I took our vacation home here instead of the house in Media. Jeff kept the place in Pennsylvania, and I decided to make Ocean City my permanent home. No kids, so it was a relatively clean break." Maddie's tone was matter-of-fact, without bitterness. "I'd always painted as a hobby, but once I moved here full-time, I started taking it more seriously. One thing led to another, and eventually, I had enough work to open this place."

"The pieces here are incredible," Lauren said sincerely. "You've really captured the essence of the shore."

"What about you?" Maddie asked. "What brings you back to Ocean City after all these years?"

"New beginnings," Lauren replied. "I needed a fresh start, and this place always held good memories. I recently took over Chipper's, our family business, and just bought a house in the Gardens. My parents retired here as well."

"No way! We're practically neighbors again. I'm in the North End."

They spent the next half hour catching up, with Lauren giving Maddie the condensed version of her recent life changes. Matt occasionally contributed to the conversation but mostly just enjoyed watching Lauren's animation as she reconnected with her childhood friend.

"This is Matt, by the way," Lauren finally said, realizing she hadn't properly introduced him.

"It's nice to meet you, Matt," Maddie said with a warm smile.

"Likewise," Matt replied. "Your work is really exceptional."

"Listen," Maddie said, "I'm having a big gallery event this Wednesday around six. I'm unveiling some new pieces I've been working on, plus featuring another local artist's work. Why don't you two come? There will be snacks and drinks. It'll be fun!"

Lauren glanced at Matt, who nodded encouragingly.

"We'd love to come," she decided. "Thank you for including us."

As they prepared to leave, Maddie gave Lauren a spontaneous hug. "I still can't believe you're back. It's like no time has passed."

Lauren returned the embrace, surprised at how comfortable it felt. "I know exactly what you mean."

Outside the gallery, Lauren and Matt resumed their stroll.

"What are the odds?" Lauren marveled, still processing the unexpected reunion. "Of all the people to run into..."

"The universe works in mysterious ways," Matt said with a smile. "She seems great—and talented."

"She is. I'd forgotten how close we were during those summers. It's strange how some friendships can just pick up again, even after decades."

CHAPTER EIGHT

Lauren stood behind the reception desk at Starfish Cove Inn, sorting through the afternoon mail. The grandfather clock in the corner ticked steadily—just past two, which meant Mrs. Calloway would soon appear for her afternoon tea. The usual quiet of midafternoon had settled over the inn, with most guests out enjoying Ocean City's attractions.

"Rosemary just finished her meditation session in the garden," Matt said, entering with a small arrangement of dried herbs and flowers that she had crafted. "She says these will 'cleanse the energy flow' or something."

Lauren smiled, making space for the arrangement on the reception desk. "Did Mr. Pemberton come back from his photography expedition?"

"Not yet. But Graham Anderson has been sitting in the parlor for three hours straight, just writing. He hasn't moved except to refill his coffee."

The front door opened, pulling their attention away from the conversation. A man wearing a navy blazer over a light-blue shirt and crisp khaki pants stepped inside. He carried a worn leather briefcase that had clearly accompanied him on many journeys.

"Good afternoon," Lauren greeted him. "Welcome to Starfish Cove Inn."

"Thank you," he replied, his voice warm and slightly gravelly. "Andrew Patterson. I believe you have a reservation for me."

"Of course, Mr. Patterson. Let me check our system." Lauren pulled up the reservations on the computer. "Yes, here you are. We have you in the Lighthouse Suite for five nights."

"Have you visited Ocean City before?" Lauren asked, retrieving his key from the cabinet behind her.

Andrew looked up, a hint of amusement in his eyes. "Many times, though not recently. I spent many summers here as a young man."

"How interesting! Has the town changed much since those days?" Lauren asked, genuinely curious about his connection to Ocean City.

"This place hasn't changed much," he remarked, his gaze lingering on the original wooden staircase. "That's refreshing."

Lauren's interest was immediately piqued. "You've been to the inn before?"

"Oh yes," Andrew replied, his expression warming with memory. "Years ago. I particularly remember that staircase—used to creak on the third step."

Lauren laughed. "It still does."

As Lauren led him upstairs to the Lighthouse Suite, Andrew moved with the deliberate pace of someone taking in details. He ran his hand along the banister, paused at a framed vintage photograph of the inn from the 1940s, and nodded appreciatively at the restored crown molding.

Just then, Rosemary emerged from her room, arms full of dried flowers. She stopped abruptly on the staircase, her eyes widening as she saw Andrew.

"Oh," she said softly. "You've brought quite an aura with you."

Andrew raised an eyebrow but smiled politely. "Have I? I hope it's a pleasant one."

"Layered," Rosemary replied, studying him intently. "Deep roots and unfinished chapters." She nodded as if confirming something to herself then continued on her way downstairs.

"One of our more… intuitive guests," Lauren explained with a small smile. "Rosemary sees the world a bit differently than most."

"Interesting woman," Andrew commented, watching her retreat.

Andrew paused at the top of the staircase, his attention caught by a sleek black shape lounging on the window seat. Binx the cat regarded him with half-lidded eyes, tail flicking lazily against the cushion. "Keeping watch over the place, are you?" Andrew murmured, extending his hand. The cat stretched before padding over to investigate the visitor.

Lauren smiled. "That's Binx, our inn cat. You'll see her around from time to time when she feels like socializing."

Lauren unlocked the door to his room, noticing how his gaze swept over every aspect of the space—the circular sitting area, the panoramic windows, the antique writing desk.

"Will this be suitable?" she asked.

"More than suitable," Andrew replied, setting his briefcase down. "I requested this room specifically, you know. The view is remarkable."

"It is one of our finest," Lauren agreed. "If you need anything at all, just let us know."

Andrew walked to the window, gazing out at the view of Ocean City. "Thank you. I have a feeling my stay here will be quite… illuminating."

Something in his tone made Lauren pause at the doorway. "May I ask what brings you back to Ocean City after so long?"

Andrew turned, a melancholy smile crossing his features. "Let's just say I have some unfinished business. Old memories to revisit."

Lauren nodded, respecting his privacy. "Well, we're happy to have you with us, Mr. Patterson. If you need anything during your stay, please don't hesitate to ask."

"Thank you. I appreciate that," Andrew replied warmly.

Lauren headed downstairs to Matt. "That new guest, Mr. Patterson? He knows the inn. Says he's been here before, years ago. Even knew about the creaky third step on the staircase."

Matt raised an eyebrow. "That's interesting. You think he might have some connection to the history we've been researching?"

"Maybe. There's something about the way he looks at everything—like he's reconnecting with an old friend rather than just staying at an inn."

"We should try to talk with him more," Matt suggested. "Without being too obvious, of course."

Their conversation was interrupted by the front door swinging open with enough force to rattle the bell. A tall woman in her early sixties strode in, her cream-colored designer suit immaculate, oversized sunglasses perched atop her perfectly coiffed jet-black hair. Behind her, a taxi driver struggled with three matching leather suitcases.

"Is this it?" the woman demanded, removing her sunglasses to reveal sharp blue eyes heavily lined with eyeliner. "When they said 'historic inn,' I was picturing something a bit more… grand."

Lauren straightened, slipping into professional mode. "Welcome to Starfish Cove Inn. How may I help you?"

"Yvonne DuBois. I should have a reservation." Her French accent was subtle but unmistakable. "The Dunes Room, I believe."

Matt stepped forward to help with the luggage while Lauren checked the system. "Yes, Ms. DuBois. We have you for six nights in our Dunes Room."

"I suppose it will have to do." Yvonne sighed, casting a critical eye around the lobby. "I usually stay at larger establishments, but I'm opening a boutique in Atlantic City next month, and I was told this little seaside town has a certain... antiquated charm."

Lauren maintained her professional smile. "We hope you'll find your stay with us comfortable. The Dunes Room has one of our finest bathrooms, including an antique claw-foot soaking tub."

"Well, let's hope the plumbing isn't also antique," Yvonne quipped, signing the registration form with a flourish.

Before Lauren could respond, the distinct sound of heels clicking against hardwood announced Mrs. Calloway's arrival. She descended the stairs with her usual regal bearing, today dressed in a pale-blue ensemble with a pearl necklace.

"Lauren, dear, is there any of that Darjeeling left? I find I need—" Mrs. Calloway stopped abruptly at the sight of the new arrival, her expression freezing in barely concealed dismay.

For a moment, the two women simply stared at each other, neither speaking. The temperature in the lobby seemed to drop several degrees.

"Victoria Calloway," Mrs. Calloway finally said, extending her hand. "Fifteen-year patron of Starfish Cove Inn."

"Yvonne DuBois," the other woman replied, accepting the handshake with obvious reluctance. "I own Maison Belle, a boutique specializing in French-inspired fashion. Perhaps you've heard of it? We have locations in Paris, New York, Philadelphia, and soon, Atlantic City."

"Can't say that I have," Mrs. Calloway replied with a tight smile. "But then, I tend to patronize establishments with more... permanence."

The tension between them was palpable. From the corner of the parlor, Graham Anderson looked up from his notebook, his pen poised mid-sentence, clearly taking mental notes of the interaction before him. Jason Hayes had emerged from the library and was watching with undisguised interest, while Lori quietly slipped a small recording device from her pocket.

"Ms. DuBois, why don't I show you to your room?" Lauren suggested, eager to defuse the tension.

"Excellent idea," Yvonne agreed, turning away from Mrs. Calloway with a dismissive sniff. "I certainly hope the accommodations are better than the company."

As Lauren led Yvonne upstairs, she could hear Mrs. Calloway announcing loudly to Matt, "I believe I'll take my tea on the porch today. The air in the lobby has become rather... stagnant."

As Lauren led Yvonne upstairs, in the hallway, they passed Rosemary, who looked between Lauren and Yvonne with interest. "Your auras are completely incompatible," she informed Yvonne matter-of-factly. "You might want to wear amethyst to soften the conflict energies."

Yvonne blinked, clearly unsure how to respond to this. "I... prefer diamonds, actually."

"Suit yourself." Rosemary shrugged, continuing down the hall.

"Is everyone at this inn so eccentric?" Yvonne asked once they reached her room.

"Our guests tend to be interesting people," Lauren replied diplomatically.

By late afternoon, just as Lauren was beginning to hope for a quiet evening, the front door chimed again. This time, a couple in their fifties entered, the woman gesturing animatedly while the man nodded with the patient expression of a long-married partner.

"Buongiorno!" the woman called out cheerfully. "Is this the Starfish Cove Inn? We made a reservation." Her English was heavily accented, her hands moving expressively as she spoke.

"Yes, welcome," Lauren greeted them. "You must be the Rossis."

"Sì, sì! I am Gina, and this is my husband, Anthony," the

woman confirmed with a broad smile. "We are touring America in our little casa on wheels"—she gestured toward a modest RV parked across the street—"but today, we decide for our anniversary week, we treat ourselves to real beds!"

Anthony, a sturdy man with salt-and-pepper hair and kind eyes, chuckled. "Three weeks in the RV, and my back, it needs a real mattress," he explained, rubbing his lower back for emphasis.

Lauren couldn't help but smile at their enthusiasm. "Well, happy anniversary! How many years are you celebrating?"

"Thirty-two years," Gina replied proudly. "We meet in cooking school in Napoli. He was the worst student," she added with a teasing wink.

"And she was the most beautiful chef in all of Italy," Anthony countered, lifting her hand to his lips. "Still is."

As Lauren checked them in, Matt entered from the hallway, wiping his hands on a dish towel. When he mentioned he had been attempting to fix a temperamental oven, Gina's eyes lit up.

"An oven problem? Anthony, get our tools from the RV. I fix many appliances in our restaurant back home."

Before they knew what was happening, Anthony had retrieved a toolbox, and Gina had followed Matt into the kitchen with the authority of a general leading troops into battle. By the time Lauren showed them to their room—the Captain's Quarters—Gina had diagnosed and repaired the oven with surprising efficiency.

"It is nothing," Gina insisted when Lauren thanked her. "In our trattoria in Milano, I fix everything myself. Why pay someone else when you have the hands to do it?" She held up her capable hands, short nails perfectly manicured despite their obvious strength.

As Lauren left them to settle in, she heard Gina already making plans.

"We must cook for them, Anthony. A proper Italian dinner to say thank you for this beautiful place."

By early evening, Lauren noticed Andrew Patterson examining the photographs in the hallway with intense interest. When she approached, he was studying a black-and-white image of the inn from the 1940s, and Jason and Lori Hayes also stood there, the two of them having an animated discussion about "historical energy imprints."

"...and this structural layout would naturally concentrate paranormal activity in the northeast corner," Jason was explaining, gesturing to the photograph.

"Finding everything all right, Mr. Patterson?" Lauren inquired, approaching the group.

The Hayes couple looked up with interest as Andrew turned, momentarily startled.

"Yes, yes. Just admiring these old photographs. This one must be from right after the war."

"It is," Lauren confirmed. "We found it in storage upstairs."

Andrew's expression flickered with what looked like recognition. "The past should inform the present, don't you think?"

"Absolutely," Jason agreed enthusiastically. "Places hold memories. Energy imprints. The very walls absorb experiences."

Andrew gave him a measured look. "An interesting perspective."

Before the conversation could continue, Matt appeared from the kitchen, his expression both bemused and slightly overwhelmed.

"Lauren, I think you need to see this. The Rossis have... Well, they've completely taken over the kitchen."

Lauren excused herself and followed Matt to discover the inn's kitchen transformed into what appeared to be an Italian culinary workshop. Gina was directing operations like a symphony conductor while Anthony methodically kneaded pasta dough. Every surface was covered with ingredients—

tomatoes, basil, garlic, olive oil, various cheeses, and several sauces simmering on the stove.

"Ah, Lauren!" Gina exclaimed, thrusting a wooden spoon toward her. "Taste this."

The flavors that exploded on Lauren's tongue were incredible—tangy tomatoes, sweet basil, the perfect balance of garlic and something deeper she couldn't identify.

"That's amazing," Lauren said after swallowing. "But Gina, you don't need to go to all this trouble."

"Nonsense!" Gina waved away the protest. "You welcome us into your beautiful inn, Anthony's back gets a proper bed, and your oven works again. Now we share our food. We just did a big grocery store visit, so it works out well. This is how we say thank you."

"We've invited all the guests," Anthony added. "The elegant ladies were... hesitant, but I think they will come."

Lauren exchanged a glance with Matt, who shrugged helplessly. There was clearly no stopping the Italian hurricane that had taken over their kitchen.

"Well, at least let us help set up the dining room," Lauren offered.

By seven o'clock, the dining room had been transformed. Lauren and Matt had set the table with the inn's best linens, vintage china place settings, and polished silver flatware. One by one, the guests arrived, drawn by the mouthwatering aromas.

The Hayes couple came without their paranormal equipment for once. Andrew Patterson entered next, followed by Mr. Pemberton with his camera. Graham Anderson brought his notebook, explaining quietly to Lauren that "dinner conversations are a gold mine for character development." Even Mrs. Calloway made an appearance along with the Whitfields.

The last to arrive was Yvonne, wearing what was obviously designer attire and looking somewhat put out to discover that the only remaining seat was directly across from Mrs. Calloway.

"Well, isn't this charming," she remarked with thinly veiled sarcasm. "How... rustic."

Mrs. Calloway's lips tightened almost imperceptibly. "The company at Starfish Cove Inn is always first-rate, Ms. DuBois. Even if our surroundings are a bit humble for your tastes."

Before Yvonne could respond, Gina burst in carrying an enormous platter of antipasti. "Sit, sit, everyone! First, we eat a little, we drink a little, we talk a little. Then pasta!"

What followed was a meal that Lauren would remember for years to come. Course after course emerged from the kitchen—bruschetta with fresh tomatoes and basil, handmade ravioli filled with ricotta, a slow-cooked ragù that Gina proudly announced had been her grandmother's recipe, and chicken piccata.

The drinks flowed freely, and with them, conversation. The Hayeses shared stories about their paranormal investigations, while Mr. Pemberton showed impressive photographs he had taken around Ocean City. Andrew Patterson contributed tales of his travels, though Lauren noticed he carefully avoided specifics about his connection to the inn.

Halfway through the meal, something unexpected happened. As Yvonne was recounting an anecdote about a fashion disaster she had witnessed in Paris, Mrs. Calloway actually laughed, a genuine laugh that transformed her usually stern features.

"The exact same thing happened to me in Milan in eighty-five," Mrs. Calloway said, leaning forward. "The poor woman's heel snapped right as she was meeting the designer!"

"No!" Yvonne gasped, delighted. "What did she do?"

"Carried on as though nothing had happened, of course. Walked the entire evening with one broken heel, her head high as a queen. I had to admire her composure."

"Dignity above all," Yvonne agreed, raising her glass in salute.

From there, the two women discovered they shared not only a passion for European travel but also for vintage jewelry and classical music, and they had a profound disdain for modern fashion's disposable nature.

"The craftsmanship in older pieces tells a story," Mrs. Calloway was saying. "This brooch was my mother's. See how the stones are set? You simply don't find that attention to detail anymore."

"Exactly!" Yvonne exclaimed. "That's why I insist on limited collections in my boutiques. Quality over quantity, always."

"These young people with their 'fast fashion,'" Mrs. Calloway said with a dismissive wave.

"Don't get me started on polyester," Yvonne replied, rolling her eyes, and both women dissolved into laughter.

Lauren caught Matt's eye across the table, both amazed at how quickly the earlier hostility had evaporated. As Andrew raised his glass in a toast to their hosts, Lauren couldn't help but notice how his gaze swept around the table, observing each guest with quiet interest.

"To Gina and Anthony, for this magnificent feast," he said. "And to Starfish Cove Inn—may her walls continue to shelter travelers and hold their stories for many years to come."

Everyone raised their glasses in agreement.

Later, as the guests began to disperse, Lauren noticed Andrew lingering in the dining room, studying the old photographs on the wall again.

"It was a wonderful evening," she said, approaching him.

"Indeed, it was," he replied, his voice soft with what sounded like nostalgia. "You know, places like this collect stories over the years. The happy ones, the sad ones. They all become part of the fabric of the building." He turned to face her. "You feel it, don't you? The history in these walls?"

Lauren nodded, surprised by his perception. "I do. Sometimes, I think the inn is trying to tell me something."

Andrew's eyes crinkled with a smile. "Perhaps it is. Old houses have ways of revealing their secrets to the right people." He glanced back at the photograph. "You just have to know where to look."

With that cryptic comment, he bid her good night and headed upstairs, leaving Lauren with the distinct impression that Andrew Patterson knew far more about Starfish Cove Inn than he was letting on.

In the kitchen, Lauren found Matt helping Gina and Anthony clean up.

"That was quite an evening," Matt said as Lauren joined them.

"Incredible," Lauren agreed. "Gina, Anthony, thank you so much."

Gina beamed with pleasure. "Food brings people together, always. Did you see those two elegant ladies? At first, they sit like this"—she demonstrated a rigid, proper posture with her nose in the air—"but by dessert, they are like old friends!"

"Food and drinks," Anthony added with a wink. "Always the best diplomacy."

CHAPTER NINE

Lauren and Matt made their way toward Asbury Avenue, where Maddie's gallery, Coastal Wonders, was hosting her latest exhibition opening. The streetlamps had just begun to flicker on, casting pools of light along the sidewalk as they approached the growing crowd outside.

"Thanks for coming with me tonight," Lauren said, glancing over at Matt. "It's nice to get out after all the chaos at the inn."

"Wouldn't miss it," Matt replied with a smile. "After the week we've had, a night of art and drinks sounds perfect."

As they approached the gallery, it became immediately clear this wasn't going to be an ordinary exhibition. Cars lined both sides of the street for several blocks, and a crowd had spilled out onto the sidewalk in front of the modestly sized building with Coastal Wonders emblazoned in elegant script above its entrance. The low thrum of music and the buzz of animated conversation drifted through the evening air.

Outside, a small bar had been set up on the patio, serving an array of colorful mocktails, Ocean City being a dry town. Guests mingled in small clusters, many dressed more formally than Lauren had anticipated.

The interior of the gallery had been transformed. Lauren and Matt had just visited Coastal Wonders a couple of days ago, but tonight, it felt like an entirely different space. The usual bright gallery lighting had been dimmed, creating an intimate atmosphere. Maddie's ocean-themed paintings lined one wall—dynamic seascapes that captured with equal skill the power and tranquility of water. But it was the opposite wall, covered entirely by a dark-blue curtain that stretched from floor to ceiling, that drew most visitors' attention.

"Lauren!" Maddie's voice called out above the crowd. She appeared moments later, weaving her way through clusters of guests. She wore a striking emerald-green jumpsuit, her hair swept up in an artful twist. "You made it! Great to see you again, Matt."

"The place looks amazing," Matt said, taking in the transformed gallery.

"The crowd is incredible," Lauren added. "Your new pieces are stunning, Maddie."

"Thank you." Maddie beamed, her eyes bright with excitement. "But wait until you see Shana's work—and what we've created together. It's going to blow your minds." She glanced at her watch. "The main event starts in twenty minutes. Grab some drinks and snacks and make sure you're near the curtain when it opens." With that cryptic instruction, she was whisked away by another guest seeking her attention.

Matt raised an eyebrow. "The main event?"

"Your guess is as good as mine," Lauren replied, accepting two bubbly drinks from a passing server. She guided Matt toward a display of Shana Durham's work, a series of abstract pieces that seemed to capture water in motion—ripples, waves, and currents rendered in shades of blue, teal, and silver. Each canvas was illuminated by a small spotlight, making the metallic elements shimmer as viewers moved around them.

"These are remarkable," Matt said, leaning closer to

examine the textured surface of one painting. "It's like she's somehow captured movement on a static canvas."

They continued through the gallery, pausing to sample the impressive spread of hors d'oeuvres set up on a long table—cheese boards with local varieties, vegetable crudités arranged in a wave pattern, and delicate seafood canapés. In the background, a DJ spun a selection of yacht-rock classics that fit the nautical theme without overwhelming conversation.

Lauren spotted several familiar faces from around town, including Mr. Pemberton from the inn, camera in hand as always, documenting the event. The room buzzed with enthusiasm, glasses clinked, and laughter punctuated the steady hum of conversation.

The lights in the gallery suddenly dimmed, causing a collective murmur of anticipation to ripple through the crowd. The DJ faded out the music, and Maddie appeared in the center of the room, a wireless microphone in hand.

"Good evening, everyone," she began, her voice carrying clearly through the now-hushed space. "Thank you all for coming to this special exhibition. As many of you know, I've been exploring ocean themes in my work for years. But recently, I've been privileged to collaborate with an extraordinary artist who shares my fascination with the deep. Please welcome Shana Durham."

A slender woman with close-cropped dark hair stepped forward, acknowledging the applause with a shy wave. Even in the dim light, Lauren could see the nervousness and excitement playing across her face.

"Together," Maddie continued, "we've created something we hope will transport you beyond the confines of this gallery, beyond the limits of traditional canvas. We want you to experience the ocean in a new way."

She nodded to someone at the back of the room, and the remaining lights faded to black. For a moment, the gallery was enveloped in complete darkness, silent except for the soft inhales of anticipation from the crowd.

Then, a single beam of soft-blue light illuminated the curtained wall. Slowly, the heavy fabric parted, revealing what appeared at first to be a massive painting of an underwater scene—a vast expanse of deepening blue, with hints of light filtering down from an unseen surface. The detail was extraordinary, capturing the subtle gradients of light and shadow in the depths.

But then the painting began to change. Delicate, translucent jellyfish materialized, drifting lazily across the scene, their tendrils trailing behind them in graceful ribbons. Their bodies pulsed with a soft bioluminescent glow. Lauren realized that these weren't painted—they were being projected onto the backdrop, moving in a hypnotically realistic manner.

A collective gasp rose from the audience as a massive whale emerged from the depths, its movement so fluid and lifelike that for a moment, it seemed as if the wall had transformed into a window to the ocean itself. The gentle giant moved with surprising grace, followed by a pod of dolphins that danced through the water with playful energy.

The illusion was complemented by a soundscape—the muffled, echoing quality of being underwater, the haunting calls of distant whales, the subtle rushing of currents. The combination of visual and auditory elements was utterly mesmerizing.

Lauren found herself holding her breath, completely transported. Matt's hand found hers in the darkness, squeezing gently as they shared the wonder of the moment.

For nearly fifteen minutes, the underwater world shifted and evolved—schools of fish darted in silver flashes, sea turtles glided majestically through their domain, and creatures from the deep rose mysteriously before disappearing back into the blue void. The projections interacted seamlessly with the painted backdrop, creating a three-dimensional effect that defied the flatness of the wall.

When the experience finally concluded, returning gradually to the initial seascape before fading to darkness, the gallery remained silent for a breathless moment. Then, as the lights slowly came back up, thunderous applause erupted. Lauren joined in enthusiastically, seeing both Maddie and Shana standing beside their creation, their faces flushed with triumph.

"That was incredible," Matt said, his voice filled with genuine awe. "I've never seen anything like it in a gallery this size. Or any gallery, for that matter."

"Me neither," Lauren agreed, making her way toward Maddie, who was now surrounded by admirers. She caught her friend's eye and gave her a thumbs-up, receiving a beaming smile in return.

As the crowd began to circulate again, the DJ resumed playing music, though at a more subdued volume that allowed the buzz of excited conversation to flow freely. Lauren and Matt drifted through the gallery, listening to snippets of enthusiastic praise for the interactive installation.

"Maddie is going to need a bigger gallery if she keeps this up," Matt commented as they refilled their champagne flutes.

"That's exactly what I was thinking," Lauren replied. When she finally managed to get a moment with Maddie, she grabbed her friend's hands excitedly. "That was absolutely spectacular. How did you even pull this off?"

Maddie laughed, her eyes bright with exhilaration. "A lot of late nights, some technical expertise from Shana's brother, who works in digital media, and a small fortune in projection equipment. Was it worth it?"

"Beyond worth it," Lauren assured her. "This is the kind of exhibition that should be getting attention way beyond Ocean City. Have you thought about social media promotion? You need someone to create some really good reels of this."

"I've been so focused on creating it that I haven't thought

much about marketing," Maddie admitted. "Do you know someone?"

"Not personally, but I can help you find the right person," Lauren promised. "This is too special not to share more broadly. It could draw visitors from all over."

By the time they left the gallery, the crowd had thinned somewhat, though plenty of guests lingered, seemingly reluctant to break the spell of the evening. Lauren and Matt walked back toward their neighborhood, the pleasant evening making for an enjoyable stroll.

"That was a pretty amazing night," Matt said, intertwining his fingers with hers.

As they made their way home, Lauren found herself still captivated by the imagery she'd witnessed. "It's like they found a way to make the paintings come alive," she mused. "I've never experienced art quite that way before."

When they turned onto their street, Matt stopped abruptly, his attention caught by the scene unfolding at the new neighbors' place. "What in the world…?"

Lauren followed his gaze and blinked in surprise. The front yard of Brian and Dina's house had been transformed into an elaborate Halloween display that hadn't been there earlier in the day. Gravestones protruded from the lawn, fog machines created an eerie mist that rolled across the grass, and the living room furniture was back on the front lawn. Multicolored lights flashed from the windows, and spooky sound effects drifted through the night air.

Most peculiar of all were the four figures seated stiffly on the misplaced furniture—two on the couch and two in armchairs—all wearing full Halloween costumes that concealed their identities completely. They sat unnaturally still, not conversing, simply staring straight ahead as if waiting for something.

"Did they set all this up while we were gone?" Lauren whispered, though they were too far away to be heard.

"Must have," Matt replied, equally baffled. "That's a lot of effort for a Halloween party with four very bored-looking guests."

As they watched, the front door swung open, and Dina emerged wearing an elaborate vampire costume, complete with a flowing cape and a mask that obscured most of her face. She carried a tray of green drinks that glowed faintly in the dim light. Taking careful steps in her impractically high-heeled boots, she made her way toward her motionless guests.

What happened next seemed to unfold in slow motion. Dina's heel caught on the edge of the front step. She lurched forward, arms pinwheeling in a desperate attempt to maintain balance. The tray tilted, sending the glowing green concoctions flying through the air in a spectacular arc before she tumbled unceremoniously onto the lawn. The scattered drinks left phosphorescent splashes across the fog-shrouded grass.

Lauren pressed a hand to her mouth, stifling a gasp. None of the costumed figures moved to help Dina. They remained eerily stationary as if they hadn't noticed her fall at all.

Brian emerged from the house a moment later, dressed as what appeared to be a mad scientist, complete with wild hair and a lab coat. He helped Dina to her feet, brushing leaves from her costume while casting anxious glances at the seated figures.

"Should we go help?" Matt asked, though he seemed reluctant to approach the bizarre scene.

Lauren hesitated, equally uncertain. "They seem to have it under control, and honestly, I'm not sure I want to get involved in… whatever that is."

As if making their decision for them, Lauren's phone buzzed with a text message. She glanced down to see Erin's name on the screen: *Are you home? You won't believe what's happening across the street.*

"Erin's watching too," Lauren told Matt, quickly typing a

response. *Just got back. Currently observing from my front yard. It's definitely... something.*

"Let's go inside," Matt suggested. "I feel like we're intruding on their strange little party, however public it may be."

They had barely settled inside Lauren's living room when a knock sounded at the door. Erin stood on the porch, bundled in a fleece jacket, her expression a mixture of amusement and bewilderment.

"Did you see that spectacular fall?" she asked as Lauren ushered her inside. "I almost felt bad for laughing, but the way those drinks went flying was straight out of a sitcom."

"We caught the whole thing," Lauren confirmed, offering Erin a seat. "Though I'm more confused by the people hanging out on the furniture. They're sitting there like statues."

Matt returned from the kitchen with three mugs of mulled wine, handing them out before settling onto the couch next to Lauren. "Maybe it's some kind of performance art? Though that fall looked pretty genuine. The whole thing is weird."

"Oh, it gets weirder." Erin leaned forward, warming her hands around the mug. "Brian and Dina were arguing all afternoon. I could hear them from my back deck. They were pacing around the yard, taking turns talking on the phone, looking really agitated."

"Arguing about what?" Lauren asked, her curiosity piqued.

"I couldn't make out most of it, but I heard phrases like 'not what we agreed to' and 'deadline extension.' Then Dina started setting up all those Halloween decorations like a woman possessed."

They fell silent, each contemplating the mystery of their peculiar neighbors. Through Lauren's front window, they could see the Halloween party continuing—Brian had set up a new tray of drinks, and the costumed guests remained as motionless as before, creating an atmosphere more unsettling than festive.

"I've lived in Ocean City my whole life," Erin said finally, "and I've never encountered anyone quite like them. And trust me, beach towns attract their fair share of eccentrics."

"It almost feels like they're playing house," Lauren mused. "Like they're pretending to be normal neighbors throwing a Halloween party but they don't quite know how it's supposed to work."

Matt chuckled. "That would explain the random furniture rearrangements and why their interactions always seem slightly off."

"Maybe they're aliens studying human behavior," Erin suggested with a grin. "And not doing a very good job of it."

They spent the next hour speculating about Brian and Dina's mysterious lives, their theories growing increasingly outlandish as the evening wore on. Outside, the strange party continued unchanged, the four guests still sitting rigidly amid the fog and flashing lights.

When Erin finally left, promising to text if anything new developed in the bizarre scenario across the street, Lauren found herself yawning despite the early hour. The day's events—from the emotional impact of the gallery exhibition to the puzzling-neighbor situation—had left her mentally drained.

"I should probably head home too," Matt said, though he made no move to leave from his comfortable position next to Lauren on the couch. "Travis and Kelly are coming to the inn tomorrow, and I want to be well-rested."

Lauren nodded, remembering their responsibilities at the inn. Yet something about the odd Halloween scene across the street made her reluctant to be alone. "Or you could stay," she suggested. "It's already late, and we're both heading to the same place in the morning."

Matt smiled, pulling her closer. "Trying to protect me from the vampire neighbors?"

"Maybe I'm protecting them from you," she countered with a laugh.

Later, as they prepared for bed, Lauren found herself

drawn to the window one last time. The strange party appeared to have concluded—the furniture was gone, the lawn cleared of decorations. It was as if the whole bizarre scene had been nothing but a strange dream.

But as she turned away, movement caught her eye. Brian stood alone in the driveway, talking urgently into a phone. Even from a distance, his body language conveyed anxiety—pacing, gesturing sharply, frequently glancing over his shoulder toward the house.

Lauren let the curtain fall back into place and headed to bed, her mind still thinking about Maddie's amazing gallery event and their neighbors' strange ways.

CHAPTER TEN

"I think that should do it," Lauren said, putting away the last of the clean dessert plates. The afternoon tea service had wrapped up at the inn, and most of the guests had dispersed to enjoy their individual activities.

"Perfect timing," Matt replied, wiping his hands on the dish towel slung over his shoulder. "I just finished in here."

Lauren headed toward the front door, ready to greet Travis and Kelly. She opened the door just as Travis was about to knock, and they both laughed at the timing.

"Welcome back to your own inn," Lauren said with a smile, stepping aside to let them in.

Kelly immediately gave Lauren a warm hug. "It's so good to see you! How's everything going?"

"See for yourself," Lauren replied, gesturing around the immaculate lobby. "Though I can't take all the credit. Matt's the real organizational genius."

Matt joined them from the dining room. "Hey, you two! How's civilian life treating you?"

Travis chuckled, clapping Matt on the shoulder. "I could get used to regular sleep and not having to make small talk at seven a.m."

"The kids are thriving with us being around more," Kelly added. "Jacob won his science competition, and we were actually there to see it."

"That's fantastic," Lauren said. "We want to hear all about it."

"First, show us around," Travis said, already glancing toward the parlor. "I'm curious what you've done with the place in our absence."

With easy camaraderie, Lauren and Matt took their friends through the inn, pointing out the small changes they'd implemented—fresh flowers in the guest rooms, a reorganized library with books grouped by genre, and the new coffee station in the lobby, which had proven popular with early risers.

"Mrs. Calloway still hanging in there?" Travis asked in a hushed tone as they passed the parlor where the formidable guest was still reading.

"She actually complimented the scones yesterday," Matt replied with a grin.

Travis's eyebrows shot up. "That's practically a marriage proposal from her."

"What about the Hayes couple?" Kelly asked. "Any ghost sightings yet?"

Lauren nodded. "They're convinced the Maritime Room has—and I quote—'unique electromagnetic properties consistent with residual paranormal energy.'"

Travis rolled his eyes while Kelly looked intrigued. "I told you that room felt different," she said to her husband, who responded with a good-natured sigh.

They ended their tour in the kitchen, where Lauren had prepared a fresh pot of coffee. The afternoon shadows were lengthening, and a gentle breeze had picked up, making the porch swing creak rhythmically.

"Why don't we take our coffee outside?" Kelly suggested. "It's such a lovely evening."

They settled into the comfortable wicker furniture on the porch, mugs in hand. From this vantage point, they could see the gardens with their fading autumn flowers and the road beyond, quiet now that the tourist season had wound down.

"So," Travis began, leaning forward in his chair, "tell us about this Midnight Supper Club you asked about. Did you find out more in the inn's records?"

Lauren exchanged a glance with Matt. "We found some old photographs and newspaper clippings about it. Apparently, it was quite the tradition here from the 1940s until the late 1990s. But we were hoping you might know more about why it ended."

Travis shook his head. "When we bought the place, the Realtor told us a little about it. But after your call, I got curious and asked around."

"And?" Matt prompted.

"And it turns out it was even more interesting than we thought," Travis continued, clearly warming to the subject. "I spoke with Eliza Carson—she owns the Sea Captain's House Bed and Breakfast on Eighth Street—and her grandparents were regular attendees in the 1950s and '60s."

"What did she say about it?" Lauren asked, leaning forward with interest.

"Well, for one thing, these weren't just ordinary dinner parties," Travis explained. "They became quite the social event in Ocean City. According to Eliza, they started simply enough during the war years—a way to share resources when food was rationed. But by the 1950s, they'd evolved into something more elaborate."

Kelly nodded eagerly. "And get this. Apparently, some real celebrities attended over the years. There were jazz musicians, a few Hollywood types, even some politicians taking a break from the spotlight."

Lauren tried to imagine the dining room filled with such

illustrious guests, the conversation and laughter flowing freely. "It must have been something special."

"From what I understand, some nights were quite fancy affairs—formal dress, gourmet food," Travis continued. "But other times, they kept things simpler. The common thread was always the midnight timing and the sense of exclusivity. An invitation to the Midnight Supper Club was apparently quite coveted in certain circles."

"Did Eliza mention anything else about why it ended?" Matt asked. "We found that article from 1997 mentioning financial considerations but wondered if there was more to the story."

Travis nodded. "Apparently, the previous owners before us, the Martins, bought the place in the nineties, and they just weren't interested in continuing the tradition. Eliza thinks they found it too much work."

"That's a shame," Lauren murmured. "It sounds like something special was lost."

"Which is why we think it's fantastic that you're considering reviving it," Kelly added. "We'd be happy to help in any way we can."

"Actually," Matt said, "we've been brainstorming ideas for the first one."

"I love that you're planning this," Kelly said enthusiastically.

They spent the next several minutes tossing ideas back and forth, the excitement building with each suggestion. Lauren could already envision the dining room transformed with decorations and food.

"Oh," Travis said suddenly as if remembering something. "That reminds me of another thing I wanted to mention. If you're interested in ideas for the inn, you should really tour some of the other historic inns in town. See how they do things, maybe get some inspiration."

"That's not a bad idea," Matt said, glancing at Lauren. "We're off tomorrow. Maybe we could check out a few places?"

Lauren nodded. "I'd like that. I've walked past the Victorian B&Bs around town dozens of times but have never been inside."

"I can make some calls," Travis offered. "Most of the owners are friends of ours, and they'd be happy to show you around. The Sea Captain's House that I mentioned is particularly interesting."

"That would be great," Lauren said. "Thanks."

The conversation drifted to other topics—the upcoming winter season, maintenance issues to watch for, and funny stories about some of the more colorful guests Travis and Kelly had hosted over the years. The evening air grew cooler as they talked, and Lauren was just about to suggest moving inside when a loud *thump* came from within the inn, followed by what sounded like footsteps.

"What was that?" Kelly asked, sitting up straighter.

Matt frowned. "It sounded like it came from downstairs. The basement, maybe?"

"Are any of the guests still inside?" Travis asked, already rising from his chair.

Lauren mentally went through the guest list. "Mrs. Calloway was in the parlor, but I thought I saw her head upstairs about twenty minutes ago. Everyone else is out, as far as I know."

Another sound echoed through the quiet inn—a metallic *clang* like a tool being dropped onto a concrete floor.

"We should check it out," Travis said, moving toward the door with Matt close behind.

They entered the inn's main hallway, which was eerily quiet now. The door to the basement stairs was located off the kitchen, a heavy wooden affair that was usually kept closed. As they approached, they could hear more shuffling sounds from below.

Travis glanced at the others then called out, "Hello? Is someone down there?"

The sounds abruptly stopped. No answer came from the darkness beyond the door.

"Maybe one of the guests went exploring," Kelly suggested, though she didn't sound convinced.

"I'll go check," Travis said, reaching for the doorknob.

"We'll all go," Matt insisted, and Lauren nodded in agreement.

Travis switched on the basement lights, illuminating the steep wooden stairs that led down into the inn's underbelly. The basement was primarily used for laundry and storage—extra linens, off-season decorations, and maintenance supplies.

Cautiously, they descended the stairs, Travis leading the way. The basement air was cooler and carried the faint musty scent that seemed common to all old buildings. The main area was relatively clean and organized, with clear pathways between the storage shelves and plastic bins labeled in Kelly's neat handwriting.

"Hello?" Travis called again. "Anyone down here?"

Silence greeted them. The only sound was the faint hum of the electric water heater in the corner.

"I don't see anyone," Lauren said, glancing around the open space. "Could it have been the pipes? This place does make some interesting noises."

"Maybe," Travis admitted, moving farther into the room. "Let's just check the whole space to be sure."

They split up, each taking a different section of the basement. Lauren examined the area near the old laundry sink, while Matt checked behind a stack of Christmas decorations. Kelly investigated the small workshop area where tools were kept, and Travis examined the furnace room.

"Nothing over here," Matt reported.

"All clear by the tools," Kelly added.

"Nothing by the furnace either," Travis said, returning to the main area. "Must have been the building settling or the pipes after all."

Lauren was about to agree when three distinct knocks sounded directly behind her—loud, deliberate, and impossible to mistake for anything mechanical. They seemed to come from the solid stone wall itself.

For a moment, no one moved, then Kelly gasped. "Did you hear that?"

"Everyone heard that," Travis said, his voice uncharacteristically tight.

Three more knocks followed, just as clear as the first set.

Lauren felt the hairs on her arms stand on end. "Okay, that was definitely not the pipes."

"Nope," Matt agreed, already backing toward the stairs. "Definitely not."

As if on cue, the overhead light flickered, plunging them momentarily into darkness before stabilizing again.

"That's it," Kelly said, her voice climbing an octave. "I'm out."

No one needed further encouragement. They rushed for the stairs, nearly colliding with each other. Lauren could have sworn she felt a cold draft brush past her as she climbed, though there was no window or vent nearby that could have caused it.

They burst through the basement door and into the kitchen before Travis slammed it shut behind them. For a moment, they all stood there, breathing heavily, staring at each other with wide eyes.

"So," Matt finally said, breaking the tense silence. "That happened."

The absurdity of the situation suddenly struck Lauren, and a giggle escaped her lips before she could stop it. Kelly followed suit, a nervous laugh bubbling up, and soon, all four of them were laughing—partly from relief, partly from the release of adrenaline, and partly from the sheer ridiculousness of four adults fleeing from mysterious knocks.

"I told you," Kelly managed between laughs, pointing an accusing finger at her husband. "I told you this place has something going on!"

Travis held up his hands in mock surrender. "Okay, okay. I admit that was... unusual."

"Unusual?" Matt echoed. "That was straight out of a horror movie! Three knocks? Come on!"

"The skeptic in me wants to say it was just the building settling," Lauren said, though she didn't sound convinced, even to her own ears.

"Three times in a row? In perfect rhythm?" Kelly shook her head. "I don't think so."

They moved to the parlor, none of them particularly eager to be near the basement door. The mutual fright had created a strange bond between them, and they spent the next hour sharing other unexplained occurrences they'd experienced at the inn. Kelly had several stories—objects moving between rooms, footsteps in empty hallways, and once, the distinct smell of pipe tobacco in the library when no one was smoking.

"Maybe this is another selling point for the Midnight Supper Club," Travis suggested, his composure mostly recovered. "Dinner and a ghost hunt."

"I'm not sure Mrs. Calloway would appreciate that," Lauren said with a smile. "Though the Hayeses would probably pay extra."

By the time Travis and Kelly prepared to leave, the incident had taken on an almost comical quality, though Lauren noticed they all kept their distance from the basement door as they passed through the kitchen.

"Let us know how the inn tours go tomorrow," Kelly said, embracing Lauren at the front door. "And thanks again for doing such a wonderful job here. We really are grateful."

"It's been our pleasure," Lauren assured her.

With final waves, Travis and Kelly departed, leaving Matt and Lauren alone in the entrance hall.

"Well," Matt said after a moment, "that was an eventful evening."

"Do you think we really heard something down there?" Lauren asked, not entirely sure she wanted the answer.

Matt considered this. "I think there are some things about this old place we don't understand yet. But whatever it was, it doesn't seem malicious. Just attention-seeking."

"Great," Lauren replied with a wry smile. "A ghost with an extrovert personality."

* * *

After ensuring all the guests were settled for the evening and the inn was locked up for the night, Lauren and Matt headed back to their respective homes. The walk was quiet, both still processing the strange events in the basement.

As they approached Lauren's house, a commotion across the street caught their attention. Red and blue lights flashed against the facades of the houses, and a large moving truck was parked in front of Brian and Dina's place. A police cruiser sat in the driveway, its occupants speaking with a middle-aged couple Lauren had never seen before.

"What now?" Lauren murmured, instinctively slowing her pace.

Erin's front door opened, and their neighbor hurried over to meet them, wrapped in a hastily donned jacket. "You're just in time for the show," she said by way of greeting, nodding toward the scene unfolding across the street.

"What's happening?" Matt asked.

"Remember our theory that there was something suspicious about our strange neighbors? They're squatters!"

"Squatters?" Lauren echoed, incredulous.

"Yep," Erin confirmed with obvious relish. "That couple talking to the police are the Moffets, the actual owners of the house. Apparently, they hired Brian and Dina's 'moving company' to relocate their belongings from Oregon while they finished up some business on the West Coast."

"Wait," Matt interjected. "So Brian and Dina were just supposed to move their stuff in?"

"Exactly!" Erin's eyes gleamed with the joy of unraveling the mystery. "But instead, they decided to move in themselves, rearrange everything, and pretend they lived there. The Moffets arrived today to find their house completely transformed, with half their furniture outside and the other half in storage."

Lauren watched as Brian and Dina emerged from the house, escorted by another police officer. They weren't in handcuffs, but their body language spoke volumes—hunched shoulders, downcast eyes, and none of the bizarre energy they'd displayed during their fake Halloween party.

"So all those strange comings and goings, the weird furniture arrangements—" Lauren began.

"They were literally playing house," Erin finished. "Moving things around, hosting fake parties, pretending to be normal suburbanites while actually living in someone else's home."

"That explains a lot," Matt said. "The furniture on the lawn must have been some of the Moffets' stuff that they didn't like."

"And those uncomfortable-looking guests at their Halloween party?" Lauren added.

"Mannequins," Erin confirmed. "The police found them in the garage. Apparently, Brian and Dina 'borrowed' them from a department store where Dina used to work."

"But why?" Lauren asked, still struggling to make sense of it all. "Why go to all that trouble instead of just, I don't know, finding an actual place to live?"

Erin shrugged. "From what I overheard, they've done this

before—moving people's belongings into new homes and then staying there themselves for a while before the owners arrive. They time it based on the moving contracts, targeting people who are relocating from far away and won't be arriving immediately."

"That's almost impressive in its audacity," Matt said, shaking his head in disbelief.

"The Moffets didn't think so," Erin replied. "Especially when they found out that Brian and Dina had been charging their credit card for 'additional moving services' this whole time."

They watched as the police officers finished taking statements, and Brian and Dina were ushered into the back of the patrol car. The moving truck began loading what appeared to be several pieces of mismatched furniture, presumably items that Brian and Dina had brought in themselves.

"Well," Lauren said as the police car pulled away, "I guess that solves one mystery, at least."

"One down, one to go," Matt replied, glancing back in the direction of the inn.

Lauren followed his gaze, thinking about the inexplicable knocks they'd heard in the basement. Between ghost stories and fake neighbors, Ocean City was proving to be far more eventful than she'd anticipated when she agreed to help run a quiet seaside inn for the offseason.

"Tomorrow's another day," she said, turning back to her home. "Maybe the inn tours will be less… dramatic."

Matt laughed. "After today? I'm not making any bets." He leaned in, pressing a soft kiss to her cheek. "Get some rest. I'll pick you up around ten for our B&B tour."

Lauren nodded, suddenly aware of Erin's interested gaze. "Sounds perfect. Good night, Matt."

"Good night," he replied, heading toward his place down the street.

"So," Erin said with a sly smile once Matt was out of earshot. "Things seem to be going well there."

Lauren couldn't help the small smile that tugged at her lips. "They are."

CHAPTER ELEVEN

"The Sea Captain's House should be just ahead on Wesley Avenue," Matt said as he drove slowly along the street, looking for parking.

"I thought it was on Central Avenue," Lauren replied, consulting the list of addresses Travis had given them.

"That's our second stop. This one is"—Matt pointed ahead as he located a parking spot—"right there."

Before them stood a stately Victorian structure painted a deep navy blue with pristine white trim. A small, tasteful sign identified it as "The Sea Captain's House, est. 1895."

"It looks so dignified," Lauren observed as Matt parallel parked in front of the building.

The front garden was meticulously maintained, with hardy autumn plantings arranged in orderly formations. The wrap-around porch featured white wicker furniture and nautical accents—ship's wheels, carefully positioned lanterns, and an antique brass telescope aimed at the distant horizon.

As they climbed the steps, the front door opened to reveal a woman in her fifties with silver-streaked dark hair and a welcoming smile.

"You must be Matt and Lauren," she said, extending her

hand. "I'm Eliza Carson. Travis called ahead. Said you're gathering ideas for Starfish Cove Inn."

"That's right," Matt confirmed, shaking her hand. "Thank you for agreeing to show us around."

"My pleasure," Eliza replied, ushering them inside. "It's always nice to connect with fellow innkeepers."

The foyer of the Sea Captain's House took Lauren's breath away. Instead of the expected nautical theme, the space was designed with an Art Deco sensibility—geometric patterns, sleek lines, and unexpected touches of gold and black. Polished marble floors gleamed beneath a striking circular rug, and a modernist brass chandelier illuminated the space. The walls featured abstract art pieces interspersed with vintage photographs of the city from different decades.

"This is incredible," Lauren said, turning slowly to take it all in.

"Thank you," Eliza replied, obvious pride in her voice. "The house was built in 1895 by Harold Wentworth, a shipping magnate who fell in love with the Art Deco movement during his travels in Europe. We've restored it to match his original vision while adding contemporary comforts."

She led them through the common areas, each room more impressive than the last. The parlor featured sleek furniture with bold angular designs and a fireplace surrounded by striking black and gold tiles.

"We've maintained the Art Deco aesthetic throughout," Eliza explained as they climbed the grand staircase to the guest rooms. "But we've also incorporated modern amenities discreetly."

This philosophy was evident in the guest rooms, where period-appropriate furniture and fixtures coexisted with hidden smart-home features. Small tablets controlled lighting, temperature, and window coverings while appearing to be vintage tabletop radios when not in use.

"The Gold Suite is our premier room," Eliza said, opening

a set of double doors at the end of the hall. "It occupies what was once Wentworth's private study."

The room was stunning—spacious with tall windows that flooded the space with natural light. The color palette featured shades of gold, black, and cream, with mosaic elements repeating in the rugs, bed linens, and window treatments. A sitting area with elegant chairs and a small writing desk occupied one corner, while the bathroom featured black-and-gold tilework with a large walk-in shower.

"It's amazing," Matt said, examining a framed map. "I can see why you're so well-reviewed online."

"We've found our niche," Eliza acknowledged. "Some guests specifically seek us out for the historical experience.

As they prepared to leave, Lauren brought up what Travis had told them earlier. "Travis said your grandparents used to attend the supper club events at our inn. We're thinking of reviving the tradition and would love any insights you might have."

Eliza's face lit up. "My grandparents loved those evenings. They always described them as magical—the combination of excellent food, interesting company, and the slightly forbidden feeling of staying up past midnight. My grandmother told me about one night in the 1960s when a jazz musician from Atlantic City showed up unexpectedly and played until dawn while everyone danced. And my grandfather always talked about the special menus, particularly a seafood feast where they served local oysters three different ways and some secret-recipe crab bisque that he still dreamed about decades later. They said there was something about sharing a meal when the rest of the world was asleep that made everything taste better and conversations more meaningful."

Lauren and Matt exchanged a glance, both clearly moved by Eliza's description.

"That's exactly what we're hoping to recapture," Lauren

said softly. "Not just serving food but creating an experience that people will remember decades later."

Matt nodded. "I think we've lost something in our world of convenience dining and rushed meals. The idea of food as an event, as something worth staying up for and lingering over, that's worth bringing back."

They thanked Eliza for the tour and set off for their next destination, The Bookworm's Retreat, located on Twenty-First Street. Where the Sea Captain's House had been sleek and glamorous, this inn proved to be cozy and intellectual.

"Welcome to the Bookworm's," greeted an older gentleman with horn-rimmed glasses and a cardigan. "I'm Howard, the owner. Travis mentioned you'd be stopping by."

The interior was every book lover's dream—a converted Victorian home where every available wall space was lined with bookshelves. Reading nooks with comfortable chairs were tucked into corners, window seats offered perfect spots for losing oneself in a story, and the scent of old books mingled pleasantly with that of fresh coffee.

"Our concept is simple," Howard explained as he showed them around. "A sanctuary for readers. No televisions, limited Wi-Fi, and over five thousand books available to borrow during your stay."

This philosophy extended to the guest rooms, each themed around a different literary genre. They toured the Mystery Room with its dark-wood furniture, vintage typewriter, and collection of classic whodunits; the Poetry Suite with its romantic décor and volumes of verse; and the Science Fiction Loft with its futuristic touches and curated collection of speculative fiction.

"Our guests come specifically for the literary experience," Howard said. "Many use their stays for writing retreats or simply to disconnect and rediscover the joy of reading without distractions."

The inn's crowning glory was its library, a two-story space

with a spiral staircase and rolling ladders that accessed the highest shelves. A massive fireplace dominated one wall, surrounded by deep leather armchairs.

"We host evening readings here," Howard explained. "Local authors, poetry slams, and discussion groups. It creates a wonderful sense of community, especially during the quieter months."

Their third stop was Rose Cottage Inn, a smaller establishment tucked away on a quiet section of Simpson Avenue. As the name suggested, gardens were the focus here, with the Victorian structure almost hidden behind meticulously maintained rose bushes, ornamental grasses, and flowering shrubs.

"Even in October, we keep things blooming," said the proprietor, Leanne, a spry woman in her sixties who greeted them like old friends. "Come February, the conservatory will be filled with forced bulbs and early bloomers. We never let a season pass without flowers."

Inside, the décor was feminine and delicate—floral patterns, pastel colors, and vintage furnishings created a sense of stepping back into a more genteel era. Each guest room was named after a different flower and decorated accordingly, from the lavender-themed Heirloom Suite to the bold-red accents of the Crimson Petal Room.

"Our specialty is afternoon tea," Margaret explained, showing them the charming tearoom with its mismatched vintage china and tiered serving plates.

By the time they left Rose Cottage, both Lauren and Matt were brimming with ideas, writing notes on their phones as they pulled the car up to their last destination, the Stardust Hotel.

"This place has a fascinating history," Matt told Lauren as they approached a grand building with a distinctive silver marquee. "Apparently, it was originally built as a small theater in the 1930s before being converted to a hotel in the fifties."

The glamorous history was immediately evident upon

entering. The lobby retained its theatrical roots with a sweeping staircase, velvet drapes, and framed movie posters from Hollywood's golden age. A stunning light fixture that resembled a cascade of stars illuminated the space.

"Several Hollywood legends stayed here during the 1950s," announced their guide, Antonio, with practiced enthusiasm. "Silver screen icons, acclaimed directors, even a few Academy Award winners. The hotel has quite the star-studded guest book."

The guest rooms continued the Hollywood aesthetic with rich fabrics, vintage fixtures, and subtle nods to classic cinema. Elegant black-and-white photographs of old movie sets adorned the walls, and plush furnishings evoked the luxury of Tinseltown's heyday.

"Our weekend movie nights are extremely popular," Antonio explained, showing them the small theater that had been preserved at the back of the building. "Every Saturday, we screen classic films, serve drinks and snacks from the era, and encourage guests to dress accordingly."

* * *

By late afternoon, Lauren's head was swimming with ideas as they headed back toward their own neighborhood.

"That was enlightening," Matt said as they drove to their homes. "Each place had such a distinct personality."

Lauren nodded, scrolling through the notes she'd taken. "It makes me think about what makes the Starfish Cove Inn special. What's our unique identity?"

"I've been pondering that too," Matt replied. "We have elements of what we saw today—some historic charm like the Sea Captain's House, some literary atmosphere like the Bookworm's—but we haven't really leaned into any one thing that makes us stand out."

"Maybe that's something to discuss with Travis and Kelly,"

Lauren suggested. "The Midnight Supper Club could be our signature offering, but we might want to develop more of an identity beyond that." She straightened suddenly in her seat, her eyes bright with excitement. "You know what? Why wait? Let's do the first Midnight Supper Club tomorrow night."

Matt glanced at her, surprised. "Tomorrow? That's awfully soon."

"For all of our current guests," Lauren clarified, already mentally planning. "I'd like to do it before Mrs. Calloway, the Hayeses, and everyone else checks out. We've grown so fond of them, and I think they'd absolutely love being part of the revival. I can make a grocery list tonight, and we can shop for food and make simple decorations tomorrow morning. Nothing elaborate, just a test run to get a feel for it but with guests who would really appreciate the experience."

"You're serious about this," Matt observed, a smile spreading across his face.

"Completely," Lauren confirmed. "After hearing Eliza's stories about her grandparents' experiences, I just feel ready now."

As they pulled onto their street, Lauren noticed a moving truck parked in front of the house formerly occupied by Brian and Dina. Two people—a man and woman—were directing movers carrying furniture inside.

"Looks like the real homeowners are settling in," Matt observed, parking in front of Lauren's place.

They had barely exited the car when the woman across the street noticed them and waved enthusiastically. After a brief exchange with the mover she'd been speaking to, she crossed the street and headed toward them.

"Hi there," she called as she approached. "I'm Jill Moffet. My husband Dean and I are your new neighbors. Well, not new-new, since we actually bought the house months ago, but new as in 'actually living here now' instead of those strange imposters."

Lauren couldn't help but smile at Jill's direct approach. With her hair in a messy bun and paint-splattered jeans, she radiated warmth and authenticity, the polar opposite of Dina's calculated perfection.

"Lauren," she replied, shaking Jill's offered hand. "And this is Matt. We live in these houses across the street," she added, gesturing to their respective homes.

"So nice to meet actual neighbors," Jill said with genuine enthusiasm. "This whole situation has been completely surreal. One minute, we're finishing up our business in Portland. The next, we're getting a call from the police saying someone's been living in our house and charging expensive furniture to our credit card."

"We witnessed some of their... unusual behavior," Matt said diplomatically. "The Halloween party with the mannequins was particularly memorable."

Jill's eyes widened. "Mannequins? Oh my, that's even worse than we thought. The police told us they'd been hosting gatherings, but I assumed they at least had real people over!"

"I'm afraid not," Lauren replied. "Though they did go to impressive lengths to make it look authentic from a distance."

Jill shook her head in disbelief. "The whole thing is beyond bizarre. Apparently, they've done this before. They operate as a legitimate moving company, identify clients who won't be arriving at their new homes immediately, and then temporarily move in themselves. According to the detective, they time it precisely, planning to be out before the real owners arrive."

"Except you arrived early?" Matt guessed.

"Exactly," Jill confirmed. "We wrapped up our business in Portland faster than expected and decided to surprise our kids with an early arrival. Instead, we were the ones who got surprised!"

Dean Moffet approached then, wiping his hands on his

jeans before offering handshakes. He was tall with salt-and-pepper hair and friendly eyes.

"The movers are asking about the bedroom furniture," he told his wife before turning to Lauren and Matt. "Hi there. I'm Dean. I see my wife has already made introductions."

"We were just hearing about your unexpected welcome to Ocean City," Lauren said.

Dean groaned. "Not exactly how we planned to start our East Coast life. Thankfully, most of our belongings are still in storage or in the moving truck. It could have been much worse."

"The detective said they mostly used our credit card to buy new furniture they liked better than ours," Jill added. "They put our stuff in storage units they rented, also with our card. The whole scheme is incredibly elaborate."

"Is everything being handled legally now?" Lauren asked.

Dean nodded. "They're facing multiple charges—fraud, identity theft, criminal trespassing. Apparently, several other homeowners have come forward with similar stories once the news broke."

"The silver lining is that everyone's been incredibly kind," Jill added. "The police, the neighbors we've met. Everyone's been so helpful and supportive."

"That's Ocean City for you," Matt said with a smile. "Despite the occasional ghost or squatter situation, it's a good community."

"Speaking of community," Jill said, her eyes lighting up, "once we're settled, we'd love to have you both over for dinner. A proper housewarming with actual human guests, not mannequins."

Lauren laughed. "We'd like that. And if you need anything in the meantime, we're right here."

After exchanging phone numbers and a few more pleasantries, the Moffets returned to directing their movers, and Lauren and Matt headed to Lauren's porch.

"They seem great," Matt said, settling into one of the chairs. "Normal, friendly people who appreciate furniture that actually looks comfortable."

"A welcome change from Brian and Dina," Lauren agreed, checking her phone as it buzzed with a notification. "Oh! It's Maddie."

Lauren opened the text message, her eyes widening as she read.

"What is it?" Matt asked, noticing her expression.

"Maddie figured out how to make social media reels for the gallery," Lauren explained, scrolling through the message. "She used some app, edited footage of the ocean installation with music and transitions, and"—Lauren looked up, excitement evident in her voice—"it's gone viral. Over a million views already!"

"That's amazing!"

"It gets better," Lauren continued, scanning the rest of the message. "A curator from a museum in New York saw it and reached out. They want Maddie to create a piece for an upcoming exhibit."

"Wow," Matt said, genuinely impressed. "That's huge for her."

"I knew she was talented," Lauren said as she set down her phone, "but this is beyond anything I expected." She couldn't keep the pride from her voice. "A New York museum exhibit. That's career-changing." Lauren glanced at her watch and stood up. "Now, to get started on the Midnight Supper Club preparation. We've got a lot to do to pull this off by tomorrow evening."

CHAPTER TWELVE

Lauren stood in the center of the inn's dining room, surveying their handiwork with a critical eye. The transformation was remarkable. What had been a charming but ordinary space hours earlier now glowed with the warm light of dozens of candles placed in hurricane lamps and vintage boardwalk-inspired lanterns. A fire crackled cheerfully in the corner fireplace, adding both warmth and a honeyed glow that complemented the candlelight. The tablecloth was a deep midnight blue, reminiscent of the ocean after sunset, with accents of copper and gold reflecting Ocean City's famous boardwalk lights.

"What do you think?" she asked as Matt arranged the last of the place settings. "Too much? Not enough?"

Matt stepped back, taking in the scene. Small glass vases held late-season coastal flowers—beach asters, golden sea oats, and scarlet sumac branches. Interspersed between them were vintage boardwalk photographs Lauren had found in the inn's collection, each mounted in a simple frame and illuminated by miniature lights. The effect was both elegant and nostalgic.

"It's perfect," Matt said, his voice warm with approval.

"You've managed to capture exactly what we talked about—Boardwalk After Dark. Sophisticated but still playful."

Lauren smiled, pleased with his assessment. The past twenty-four hours had been a whirlwind of activity as they prepared for the inaugural Midnight Supper Club. After their tour of Ocean City's historic inns the day before, inspiration had struck hard and fast. They'd spent the morning shopping for ingredients and decorations, transforming the dining room throughout the afternoon and preparing the menu between regular inn duties.

"I just hope the food turns out as well as the decor," Lauren said, glancing toward the kitchen, where her creations were already filling the air with the aroma of herbs and melting cheese.

"It will," Matt assured her, straightening the last fork. "Everything is coming along perfectly."

The menu they'd devised was a playful reimagining of Ocean City boardwalk classics. Lauren's handcrafted gourmet pizzas featured a thin, crisp crust topped with heirloom tomatoes in a rich garlic-infused olive oil, creamy buffalo mozzarella, fresh basil, and a drizzle of aged balsamic reduction. Matt had prepared an elevated version of boardwalk fries to accompany homemade crab cakes. For dessert, they'd created individual funnel cakes with seasonal fruit compote and hand-whipped cream.

For drinks, they offered a selection of boardwalk-inspired beverages: fresh-squeezed lemonade with mint and berries, craft sodas, sparkling waters infused with seasonal fruits, and a variety of hot teas for those feeling the autumn chill.

"The porch looks beautiful too," Lauren said, moving to the French doors that opened onto the wraparound veranda. Outside, more hurricane lamps cast a golden glow over comfortable seating areas draped with soft blankets to ward off the October chill. The railing held a string of warm white lights that mimicked the boardwalk's famous illumination.

"I think we're all set," Matt said, checking his watch. "It's almost eleven. Should we start getting ready ourselves?"

Lauren nodded. They'd decided to dress for the occasion, wanting to honor the formality that had marked the original Midnight Supper Club gatherings they'd seen in the old photographs.

Thirty minutes later, Lauren descended the stairs in a simple midnight-blue dress that complemented the evening's theme. She'd left her hair down but had swept one side back with a vintage silver clip. Matt waited at the bottom of the staircase, looking handsome in dark slacks and a crisp white shirt with a subtle green tie that brought out the color of his eyes.

"You look beautiful," he said, his gaze appreciative as she joined him.

"Thank you," Lauren replied, a slight flush coloring her cheeks. "You clean up pretty well yourself."

The sound of footsteps from the hallway drew their attention. Andrew Patterson appeared, impeccably dressed in a navy blazer with a pocket square that somehow managed to look both timeless and contemporary.

"Well, don't you two look splendid," he said, his eyes crinkling at the corners. "I must say, when you mentioned reviving the Midnight Supper Club, I wasn't expecting such attention to historical detail."

"We were inspired by the photographs we found," Lauren explained. "It seemed like such a special tradition."

Andrew nodded, his expression thoughtful. "It was indeed. I remember my grandmother telling stories about these gatherings when I was a boy."

"Your grandmother?" Matt asked, his interest piqued.

Before Andrew could elaborate, more guests began to arrive. The Hayes couple appeared, having temporarily abandoned their ghost-hunting equipment in favor of evening attire. Jason wore a tweed jacket with elbow patches that made him look like a professor, while Lori had chosen a period-style dress that perfectly suited the evening's nostalgic theme.

"This is exactly how I imagined the inn would have looked in its heyday," Lori said, gazing around the transformed space with obvious delight. "The energy is completely different tonight. Can you feel it, Jason?"

Jason nodded eagerly. "Absolutely. There's a resonance to the space that wasn't present before. I'd wager we're tapping into the historical memory of the building itself."

Graham Anderson arrived next, notebook conspicuously absent for once, though Lauren suspected he was mentally recording every detail. Rosemary floated in wearing a flowing dress with multiple scarves draped artfully around her shoulders, immediately commenting on the "harmonious vibrational frequency" of the candlelight.

To Lauren's surprise, Mrs. Calloway made her appearance, elegant as always in a tailored ensemble that somehow managed to be both formal and practical for the late hour.

"I generally don't approve of dining after eight," she announced as Matt offered her a glass of sparkling elderflower water, "but I suppose traditions must be respected."

"We're honored you could join us," Lauren said sincerely.

Mrs. Calloway's expression softened momentarily. "Well, I couldn't very well miss what promises to be the social event of the season, could I?"

The Rossis entered with their characteristic enthusiasm, Gina gushing over the decorations while Anthony complimented Matt on the aromas emanating from the kitchen. They were followed by George Pemberton, who had abandoned his usual photography gear but couldn't resist bringing a small vintage camera "to document the occasion."

The Whitfields arrived arm in arm, Chloe looking radiant in a simple cream-colored dress. "When you mentioned a midnight supper, I thought it sounded romantic," she told Lauren. "But this is beyond what I imagined."

Last to arrive was Yvonne DuBois, fashionably late and dressed impeccably in what was undoubtedly a designer outfit. To Lauren's amusement, she immediately gravitated toward Mrs. Calloway, the two women falling into conversation about a mutual acquaintance they'd discovered during the Rossis' impromptu dinner.

As the guests mingled around the table, Binx made her ceremonial appearance, padding silently into the dining room with the dignity of a maitre d' inspecting the evening's arrangements. The black cat paused at the threshold, her golden gaze reflecting the candlelight as she surveyed the gathering. She wound her way between chairs, accepting gentle strokes from the guests before finding a perfect vantage point on the windowsill. From there, she could observe the proceedings with feline approval.

"Shall we begin?" Matt suggested once everyone had taken their seats, each with a specialty beverage in hand.

Lauren nodded and cleared her throat. "Thank you all for joining us tonight for the revival of the Starfish Cove Inn's Midnight Supper Club. This tradition began during World War II and continued for over fifty years, bringing together visitors and locals for conversation, connection, and celebration. When Matt and I discovered the photographs and articles about these gatherings, we knew immediately that we wanted to bring this tradition back."

Matt raised his glass of lemonade. "Our theme tonight is Boardwalk After Dark, a celebration of Ocean City's famous landmark and the special place where we've all found ourselves gathered this October. So here's to new traditions built on old foundations, to connections made across time, and to a magical night at Starfish Cove Inn."

Glasses clinked as everyone echoed the toast, and the evening officially began. Lauren and Matt moved between the kitchen and dining room, serving the first course while conversation flowed easily around the table. To Lauren's delight, the group dynamics were fascinating—Mrs. Calloway and Yvonne continuing their unexpected friendship, the Hayes couple drawing Andrew into a discussion about the inn's architecture, and Rosemary explaining something involving "energy meridians" to a politely bewildered George Pemberton.

As they served the main course, Lauren noticed Andrew studying the room with particular intensity, his gaze lingering on certain architectural details.

"Mr. Patterson," she said, refilling his water glass, "you mentioned something earlier about your grandmother's stories of the Midnight Supper Club. Were you a frequent visitor to Starfish Cove Inn?"

The table quieted somewhat, other conversations pausing as guests turned with interest toward Andrew.

"Not as frequent as I would have liked," he replied, setting down his fork. "But yes, I spent many summers here as a boy in the 1960s. My grandmother ran the inn until I was about twelve." He glanced around at the expectant faces. "I suppose now is as good a time as any to share my connection to this place. My full name is Andrew Patterson Matthews."

A murmur went around the table.

"Matthews? As in Evelyn Matthews?" Matt asked, recognition dawning. "The woman who converted this house into an inn after her father disappeared?"

Andrew nodded, a smile playing at the corners of his mouth. "Evelyn Matthews was my grandmother. I was fortunate enough to experience the Starfish Cove Inn during its golden years, how she transformed her family home into a gathering place for travelers and locals alike during some of the most challenging years in American history."

"That's extraordinary," Lauren said, genuinely moved by the revelation. "No wonder you seemed so at home here from the moment you arrived."

"I recognized you the minute you walked in," Rosemary announced, to everyone's surprise. "Your energy signature is imprinted all over this building. You're connected to its very foundation."

For once, no one seemed inclined to dismiss Rosemary's unusual observations.

"Why didn't you say anything when you first checked in?" Mrs. Calloway asked, direct as always.

Andrew's smile turned wistful. "I wanted to experience the inn as it is now, to see how it's evolved. My grandmother sold this place long before she passed away, and I'd never returned until now. I've been traveling extensively for work most of my adult life, but recently..." He paused. "Recently, I've been thinking about roots, about connections to the past."

"And what do you think of how the inn has changed?" Chloe asked, genuine curiosity in her voice.

"I think my grandmother would be delighted," Andrew replied without hesitation. "The essence of what she created is still very much alive here. Especially tonight." He raised his glass in Lauren and Matt's direction. "This gathering—strangers becoming friends over good food and conversation—this was exactly what she envisioned when she started the Midnight Supper Club."

The conversation expanded from there, with Andrew sharing stories of his grandmother's determination to keep the inn running through rationing and shortages during the war years. "She started the suppers as a way to pool resources," he explained. "Everyone would bring what they could—a bit of sugar here, fresh vegetables from a victory garden there. Together, they created meals that none of them could have managed alone."

"That's the true spirit of hospitality," Anthony observed. "Making something wonderful from whatever is available."

Gina nodded enthusiastically. "In our village in Italy, this is how we always cook. Everyone brings something. Everyone shares."

As Matt served dessert—the promised funnel cakes, delicate and crisp, artfully arranged with seasonal fruit—Andrew continued his storytelling, recounting how his grandmother had welcomed returning soldiers, creating a safe haven where they could readjust to civilian life.

"She believed in the healing power of community," he said. "That sharing a meal with others was about more than just food. It was about creating a space where people could truly be present with each other."

Lauren felt a profound sense of connection as she looked around the table. In just a couple of short weeks, these people had become important to her, not just as guests at an inn she was temporarily managing but as individuals whose stories and personalities had enriched her life in unexpected ways.

As midnight passed and conversation continued to flow, Lauren caught Matt's eye across the table. He smiled, clearly feeling the same sense of accomplishment and rightness that she was experiencing. Somehow, in reviving this tradition from the inn's past, they had created something meaningful for everyone present.

It was Jason Hayes who first noticed it, glancing out the window during a lull in conversation. "Is that... Are those the Northern Lights?"

Everyone turned toward the windows, where an unmistakable green glow was visible in the night sky.

"It can't be," Mrs. Calloway said, though she was already rising from her seat. "The aurora borealis isn't visible this far south."

"It is tonight," George said, already reaching for his camera. "There was a massive solar flare earlier this week. The news mentioned it might create unusually strong auroras, visible much farther south than normal."

They migrated to the porch as a group, specialty drinks and dessert plates temporarily forgotten as they witnessed the extraordinary sight. Ribbons of green, purple, and pink light danced across the northern sky, reflecting off the ocean.

"In all my years visiting Ocean City, I've never seen anything like this," Mrs. Calloway murmured, momentarily dropping her usual reserve.

"It's a sign," Rosemary said confidently. "A cosmic alignment to bless this gathering."

"We should get down to the beach for a better view," Jason suggested excitedly. "Without the town lights, the display will be even more spectacular."

The suggestion prompted a division of the group. The older guests—Mrs. Calloway and Yvonne—opted to remain on the porch with its comfortable seating and protection from the brisk October wind. The others, however, were eager to experience the phenomenon from the open beach.

"We'll bring blankets and pillows," Lauren suggested, already heading inside to gather supplies.

Minutes later, a procession made its way down the street toward the boardwalk—Matt and Lauren leading the way, followed by the Hayes couple, Andrew, the Whitfields, the Rossis, Graham, George, and Rosemary, all carrying blankets and extra layers against the night chill.

The boardwalk was nearly deserted at this hour, creating an almost magical atmosphere as they walked along the wooden planks, the ocean to their right, the darkened storefronts to their left, and above them, the extraordinary light show painting the sky in otherworldly colors.

"It's like something from a dream," Chloe whispered, leaning against her husband as they walked.

They found a perfect spot on the beach, away from the boardwalk lights but still with the familiar silhouette of Ocean City as their backdrop. Blankets were spread on the sand, and they settled in small groups, all gazing upward at the celestial display.

George positioned his camera on a small tripod, capturing long-exposure shots of the aurora, while the Hayes couple debated whether the Northern Lights had any paranormal properties. The Rossis sat close together, Anthony's arm around Gina's shoulders as they murmured to each other in Italian. Andrew wandered along the edge of the gathering, occasionally stopping to point out particularly vibrant bursts of color to the others, his usual reserve softened by genuine wonder. Graham Anderson sat slightly apart, his expression contemplative as he absorbed the experience, undoubtedly filing it away for a future novel.

Lauren and Matt found themselves at the edge of the group, sharing a large blanket.

"I'd say our first Midnight Supper Club was a success," Matt said softly, his gaze still directed at the sky.

"Beyond what I could have imagined," Lauren agreed. "Did you see everyone's faces when Andrew revealed who he was? That moment alone was worth all the preparation."

"And now this," Matt added, gesturing toward the aurora. "Talk about a perfect ending."

They sat in comfortable silence for a few moments, the only sounds the crash of waves and the occasional murmur of conversation from the others.

"You know," Matt said finally, his voice quiet enough that only Lauren could hear, "when Travis first asked us to help with the inn, I never expected it would lead to... this."

"This light show?" Lauren asked, though she knew that wasn't what he meant.

Matt turned to face her, his expression earnest in the strange, shifting light. "This feeling. Like I've found something I didn't even know I was looking for."

Lauren felt her heart quicken. "I know exactly what you mean. These past weeks have been... transformative."

Matt's hand found hers on the blanket, his fingers intertwining with her own. "It's not just the inn, though. It's you, Lauren. Working together, creating this evening, seeing how naturally we complement each other... It feels right in a way I wasn't expecting."

Lauren squeezed his hand, a warmth spreading through her that had nothing to do with the blanket they shared. "For me too."

"Look," Matt whispered, pointing toward the horizon where the green lights seemed to be intensifying. "It's getting stronger."

Lauren followed his gaze but found herself looking at his profile instead—the strong line of his jaw, the wonder in his expression, the way the aurora's light played across his features. In that moment, she felt a certainty settle over her, a sense of possibility she hadn't experienced in a long time.

Matt turned, catching her gaze, and smiled. Without words, he shifted closer, and Lauren leaned her head against his shoulder as they returned their attention to the sky, where curtains of light continued their cosmic dance above Ocean City.

In the strange, beautiful glow of the aurora, with the sound of the ocean as their soundtrack and surrounded by new friends, Lauren felt a sense of belonging more profound than anything she'd experienced since moving to Ocean City. It was, she realized, exactly what Evelyn Matthews had created all those years ago—a space where connections were formed, where strangers became friends, and where magic could happen at midnight.

EPILOGUE

November arrived with a chill that settled into Ocean City's bones. The boardwalk stood mostly empty, the shops closed for the season, shutters drawn tight against the advancing winter. Starfish Cove Inn had settled into its off-season rhythm—a steady trickle of weekend guests, business travelers passing through, and the occasional romantic-getaway seeker drawn by the promise of seaside solitude.

Lauren stood at the kitchen window, watching gray clouds gather over the Atlantic, promising rain later that evening. Behind her, the oven timer chimed, and she pulled out a batch of cranberry-orange scones that filled the room with a warm, citrusy aroma.

"Those smell wonderful," Matt said, entering with an armful of firewood. He deposited the logs in the copper bin beside the parlor fireplace and brushed a few stray leaves from his sweater. "The fire in the parlor is going strong, and Mrs. Hopkins is happily settled with her mystery novel and tea."

The November wind rattled the windows, and Lauren pulled her cardigan tighter as she moved away from the drafty pane.

The phone rang, and Matt reached for it. "Starfish Cove

Inn, Matt speaking." His expression brightened. "Hey, Travis! How's the family?"

Lauren moved closer, eager to hear any news. Since the inaugural Midnight Supper Club and the extraordinary night of the Northern Lights, they'd held one more successful gathering just last week, a Harvest Moon dinner that had drawn not only returning guests but also a bunch of locals who'd heard about their revival of the historic tradition.

Matt put the call on speaker so Lauren could join the conversation.

"We've been thinking," Travis was saying, his voice filling the kitchen. "Kelly and I usually keep the inn open through the holidays, but this year, we're considering closing from December twentieth through New Year's. Bookings are practically nonexistent anyway, and the kids have been begging for a proper family Christmas without guest check-ins. Frankly, you two have earned a break as well."

Lauren and Matt exchanged glances, a silent communication passing between them.

"Actually," Matt said slowly, "we were hoping to experience Christmas at the inn. Lauren and I were just talking about it yesterday—the possibilities for decorations, special breakfasts, maybe even reviving some old holiday traditions we found in those record books."

"Really?" Travis sounded surprised. "You want to work through the holidays?"

Lauren leaned closer to the phone. "Matt and I both love Christmas, and the idea of creating something special here at the inn, well, it just feels right."

"And honestly," Lauren continued, "I think the inn would book up quickly. The Midnight Supper Club has generated such positive word of mouth. I've already had several guests ask if we'd be open for Christmas."

There was a pause on the line, followed by muffled conversation as Travis presumably consulted with Kelly.

"If you're serious," Travis said when he returned, "we could actually open up the bookings. We've had quite a few inquiries already that we've been turning away. It could be good for business, and the kids could still have their family Christmas at our house while you manage the inn."

"We're completely serious," Lauren assured him. "Between the two of us, we can handle it. And honestly, the idea of a Starfish Cove Christmas is too magical to pass up."

By the time the call ended, it was settled. Travis would reopen the Christmas week bookings immediately, and Lauren and Matt would have free rein to create the holiday experience they envisioned.

As Matt hung up the phone, Lauren could already see the possibilities unfolding—the Victorian decorations that would transform the spaces, the special menus they could plan, the holiday-themed Midnight Supper Club gathering on Christmas Eve.

"You're sure about this?" Matt asked, studying her expression. "It will be a lot of work."

Lauren put her arm around Matt's shoulders. "I've never been more sure of anything. Just think of it—a Christmas tree in every room, garlands on the staircase, holiday music in the parlor. We could have cookie decorating in the afternoons, hot chocolate on the porch..."

Matt laughed. "I can already see you've got it all planned out."

The gray November sky darkened outside, and a light rain began to tap against the windows, transforming the afternoon into a cozy haven of warmth and comfort within the inn's walls. Lauren closed her eyes for a moment, imagining the inn dressed in its holiday finest, fragrant with pine and spices, filled with the laughter of guests experiencing the magic of Christmas by the sea.

"Christmas at Starfish Cove," Matt murmured as if testing the words. "It has a nice ring to it."

* * *

Pick up book 4 in the Ocean City Tides Series**, An Ocean City Christmas,** to follow Lauren, Matt, and the rest of the bunch.

Have you read the Cape May Series? If not, start with book 1, **The Cape May Garden**.

ABOUT THE AUTHOR

Claudia Vance is a writer of women's fiction and clean romance. She writes feel good reads that take you to places you'd like to visit with characters you'd want to get to know.

She lives with her boyfriend and two cats in a charming small town in New Jersey, not too far from the beautiful beach town of Cape May. She worked behind the scenes on television shows and film sets for many years, and she's an avid gardener and nature lover.

Copyright © 2025 by Claudia Vance

All rights reserved.

No part of this book may be reproduced in any form or by any electronic or mechanical means, including information storage and retrieval systems, without written permission from the author, except for the use of brief quotations in a book review.

This is a work of fiction. Names, places, events, organizations, characters, and businesses are used in a fictitious manner or the product of the author's imagination.

Made in the USA
Middletown, DE
04 August 2025